PUBLISHED BY

Carolina Comfort Press

New Bern, NC 28560   (252)514-2953

Printed in the United States of America

ISBN 978-0-9707197-9-9

Karen Dodd took and enhanced all pictures in this book.
www.karenedodd.net

Carl Hultman's artistic talents completed the cover.
www.carlhultman.com

BEAR WITH ME, DEAR

Karen Dodd

Thank you all.

Some of this book is true. Most is fiction and I've rearranged things a bit. I love talking about my home of choice, New Bern, NC and all the history that has pumped through its heart in the past 300 years. The people, especially the not so nice ones, are definitely fiction, so don't go looking in the phonebook to find their addresses. Most of the places are real, even the Bones on the Trent River! Most nice folks do welcome your attention, but Fiona and family are fiction. I even made up her home. I want to thank a few people and give mention to a few more.

I thank Jean and Carl Hultman for their encouragement and help, Richard Farrow for giving me the name of Semper Fi when I needed it, also Victor Jones, John Green, John Leys at the New Bern Library for their gossip, research and time. The Firemen's Museum, Mrs. Mohr, Pat Traynor, NB Historical Society, Earl of Craven Questers: Annette Hunt, Nancy Mansfield, Alice Ruckart were all there when I needed a question answered. If you want to schedule your own Quester Luncheon call Dottie Webb 252-638-3529.

My appreciation goes to all the homeowners whose homes are pictured in these pages, NC Business History website for information on Gilbert S. Waters, Bear D'Olde Towne, GeeVee Meyer, Community of Olde Towne for allowing me permission to use their very proper BEAR on this cover. Thank you Craven Arts Council, Barbara Lubsen, the artists and *all* the Bear Town Bears, LLC, NC History Center at Tryon Palace and Margaret Rose of Neuse Realty for a little realty research. As always, I appreciate Denton Dodd,

Rosie Wood, Delle Curry and Christine Grotheer for their editing eyes and the wonderful folks at Lightning Source Publishing who helped make this book possible.

For any mistakes and errors in this book, I apologize. Some things I fiddled with to make the story, some things I added and some things slipped through my mind. Enjoy it anyway.

Now comes the fun part. I want you to visit and see New Bern streets as I have during the past few years. In the text of this book, I included house pictures and named them #1-10.

The first 10 people who write me the correct addresses of those houses get a free book! I have eight published books and all you have to do is give me the street number of each house with your name, address and name the book you would like to own.

BEAR WITH ME, DEAR

Chapter 1

"Mama, is that Ms. Henrietta? Good Lord, she has to be as old as Methuselah by now!" My younger daughter, Lucy, was visiting for a couple of weeks while her husband, Sam Gaskill, attended an Atlanta banking conference. Her blonde and red highlights brushed her face as she swirled her head and looked at me. "I mean, she was old when I was a little girl." Lucy wrinkled her nose as she pulled her pink knit sweater off and tied it around her waist. We stood at the corner of George and Pollock Streets in front of the Tryon Palace gates.

The woman in question, Henrietta Gay Simmons, turned in front of us and scurried across the street. She wore thick-heeled navy laced shoes, seamed dark stockings, which went out in the '50s, and a paisley print shirtwaist with a little white lace collar. A gold chain across the front of her throat clasped a hand knitted sweater around her shoulders. It had been her standard uniform for as long as I could remember. Ms. Henrietta was the Grand Dame of New Bern, North Carolina. She had been chair of the Women's Club, Regent of the DAR, president of the garden club and the ladies of the church.

Her unflappable impressions and opinions have swayed every organization in town for the past 50 years. This morning the squashed navy straw hat perched on her head dangled a pale pink rose from one side. The breeze caught the hat's netting and flipped it backward over her head like a wind scoop.

Henrietta Gay left the Commission House and headed over to the ticket office at the Tryon Palace Gardens and Tours. From the look on her face, I could tell there was a bee in her bonnet, as well as that squashed rose. "Oh yes, as busy as always with her nose in everyone else's business." I'm a retired schoolteacher, who used to volunteer at the Tryon Palace Shop and Gardens, a local tourist attraction. Last winter, I helped open the new NC History Center on the waterfront at Tryon Palace and closed the previous gift shop, which stood behind us on the corner of George and Pollock Streets.

Since our new boat purchase, I don't have time to volunteer at Tryon Palace, the reconstructed 18th century governor's home. "But here comes the trolley." While Lucy visited, I decided to reacquaint myself with some of the popular tourist attractions and events in town. That morning we stood in line at the trolley stop in front of Tryon Palace. New Bern's previous trolley ran on a railway around town. This version wheeled around on tires and ran like a bus, with open-air sides, but appeared to be an old-fashioned trolley.

The driver parked the vehicle at the curb and leaned back in his seat. Another gentleman descended the steps. I was delighted to see an old acquaintance would be our guide for the day. Geoffrey Bottoms was a retired doctor, very involved in New Bern historical activities. "Good morning, Fiona Wade. I haven't seen you in a while. Found any new bodies lately?"

"Lord, I hope not. I've found enough dead bodies to last a lifetime. That last one was a doozy." Unfortunately, in my retirement, I felt like Jessica Fletcher's sister-in-crime solving. In the past year, I've helped solve a couple of murder cases here in town. At my husband's urging. I have retired, not only from teaching, but also from sleuthing. "You know, Geoffrey, we bought a boat last year. This warm winter allowed us to take a few trips up the river and back."

BEAR WITH ME, DEAR

We live at the junction of two rivers here on the coast of North Carolina, the Trent and the Neuse. This area, known as North Carolina's Inner Banks, is not as well known as the more familiar Outer Banks. Our rivers run into sounds, the sounds, into the ocean. "There are a lot of good boating places to consider. It's kept me busy enough.

"So, no Geoffrey, in answer to your question, I'm no longer in the body-finding business. I just want to enjoy our boat, our family and retirement.

"I don't know if you remember her, but this is our daughter, Lucy Burgin. She lives in Swansboro and is visiting for a couple of weeks." Most Southern women have double names and our Lucy Burgin is no exception. I stepped back, so that Lucy could shake his hand. While she was doing that, she slipped him some folded bills to cover the cost of our tour.

"Well, yes, I do remember you, but the last time I saw you, you were just a little bit of a girl. You sure grew up all pretty." Geoffrey helped her climb into the trolley and then held my hand as I took a step up.

"Which side Mama? Will we see more stuff on the right side or the left?"

"It doesn't matter; there is good stuff to see on both sides." I took a seat on the aisle while Lucy moved toward the window and pulled out her camera. In 15 minutes, the trolley was full, and we rolled up the street as Geoffrey pointed out this house or that building and recounted its history. He has an amusing way with words. New Bern, being over 300 years old, has a lot to show off - the architecture, the wars, the people and the always "moving homes."

Between Tryon Palace and the Historical Society buying up old homes and placing them on new properties, we acquired the nickname of the Town of the Moving Homes.

Toward the end of the tour, we stopped at Cedar Grove Cemetery and strolled down the oyster shell lanes as we peered at the headstones and into mausoleums.

We gathered just outside the gates before we left. "Did anyone feel a drop of water as you went under the archway?" Geoffrey smiled, as we all climbed back on the bus. "It's said that anyone who feels the wall weep, will be the next one to enter – forever."

He paused; his bushy eyebrows did a quick dance above his bright blue eyes.

He continued, "The archway weeps because of the material it was cut from. The marl is similar to the coquina stone one might find in Florida. You can't find rock if you dig deep, but the marl is mined. Cut in blocks, it serves as a building material; ground up it becomes a fertilizer. There is a quarry and phosphate mine up in Aurora, not far from here." His large hand reached out to grasp the overhead rail as the bus pulled forward. "It's just a rumor, we call it a *grave* joke, that if you feel a drop as you pass under the gate, you'll be back – in a box carried by six friends." He gave a sinister snigger.

A tiny shiver ran up my body, as I leaned back on the bench. Dear Lord, I didn't want to hear about anyone dying anytime soon.

BEAR WITH ME, DEAR

Cedar Grove Marl Arches

Chapter 2

Lucy and I returned home from our trolley tour. Just as we were sitting down and propping up our feet, the phone rang.

"Fiona Wade, didn't I catch a glimpse of you on the trolley this morning?" Henrietta Gay Simmons' voice grabbed at me through the telephone receiver, grating my nerves. I shrank down, shutting my eyes as I listened to her voice. "I wish I had time to be chauffeured around town with nothing on my mind."

I didn't lower myself to explain I was hosting a guest, not that it was any of the old busybody's business. "Why Ms. Henrietta, yes, I remember seeing you. You seemed to be in a hurry. I didn't stop you to say hello."

"I wonder if you would do the Women's Club a favor and pick up some brochures and posters for the Spring Homes Tour." I could hear her dentures click between breaths. "You live downtown and, being so close, I know you wouldn't mind delivering some posters and information to all the downtown businesses." She paused, knowing I couldn't deny her request.

"I, myself, take an evening stroll every day to keep up my energy and stay in good form. Perhaps you could enjoy the same by taking a bit of a walk for me." Was she insinuating I needed to be in better shape? The old biddy had no idea I walked about every day and Gerald, my Dear Husband, thought I was just the right size!

After biting my tongue, I responded, "Just tell me where to pick them up and when you'd like them out, Ms. Henrietta."

"Come collect them at my house off Country Club Lane and the sooner, the better. If I'm not here, I'll leave them on the bench by the front door with a list of suggested businesses for their placement." She hung up on me. No *please* or *thank you* or even a *fare thee well*. I imagined the prim old woman putting down her receiver and with it, all thoughts of the good deed she requested of me.

As it happened, I was driving Lucy down to show her Nicholas Sparks' house that afternoon. Henrietta's house was on the way. I turned to my younger daughter and said, "Anything else you want to do, while you're here?" I slid the list of potential tourist options for New Bern and then poured myself a cup of coffee.

"Nope, I think we covered it all. What time do Beverly's kids get home?" She looked at her watch. She knew we watched out for them and drove them to their after school activities or whatever needed to be done until Beverly Jane or her husband Bart arrived home. "I'd like to see them before we go."

I thought about the older daughter, with her rigid rules, dark hair and structured business suits, comparing her to my younger Lucy, blond, relaxed, always smiling -- and childless. "They should be coming in pretty soon, anytime after 3:30. That gives us time to go upstairs and watch the river if you like?"

"Sounds good." She stirred cream into her coffee mug and climbed the stairs ahead of me. The second floor of our carriage house contains another bedroom, a bathroom and opens onto a large and well-used deck that overlooks the junction of the two rivers and their bridges as well as every evening's sunset.

Gerald, my Dear Husband, was sitting in one of my periwinkle blue Adirondack chairs, finishing a puzzle he started that morning. "Hey, Sugar. We're so glad you came to visit us this week. Your mom and I don't get to see you that much."

"Oh, Daddy, I call, don't I? It's just that Sam and I get to working on a project and then decide to take off for the weekend and well... You're right. We are pretty flighty about family obligations." She bit the inside of her mouth, like she did when she was a child with a thought on her mind. "Mama, how old were you when you had me?" That question came out of the blue for sure.

Uneasy with where that conversation might lead, Gerald shifted forward in his chair and stood up. "I'm going down to fix me some fresh coffee and maybe make a few chocolate chip cookies. I'll bring them up when they're done." My Dear Husband retreated to a safer region of the house.

"I was 38 and you were the *only* planned child. We were older and established in our work. We felt like we wanted to try one more time. Beverly Jane and Hancock were well out of diapers by then. We wanted another baby." I smiled hoping she would say more. "I'm glad we did. You are very special."

When she didn't elaborate further, I picked up my knitting. "What makes you ask?" Having been a teacher for many years, I know the benefits of asking an open-ended question.

Lucy picked at a non-existent cuticle and then glanced over to the river before she took a deep breath. "I wondered if I've waited too long, before having my first. They say older women have more complicated pregnancies. I've been on the pill so long and don't know if I can get pregnant. Sam and I have enjoyed our 'freedom,'" she made rabbit ears with her fingers, "for ten years. We started talking about having children a couple of months ago. Frankly, it frightens me."

I held my breath, not wanting to break this special out-loud sharing.

"I mean we both have good jobs. We bought the house thinking there was room for children … and we have a good savings if I have to stop work. In fact, I was thinking of starting my own business and working from home." Her degree was in interior design, but she wasn't driven like our oldest child, Beverly.

Currently, Lucy worked for a contractor selecting fixtures, colors, floorings and wallpaper in his developments. The one growing area in eastern North Carolina was around the Marine Corps bases at Cherry Point and Camp Lejeune. She had a gift for the business and a good eye for color.

Lucy helped me decide on what colors and fixtures to choose when we built our little carriage house a couple of years before. "I think you'd be very good as both a mother and a home business owner. At first, a child will take a lot of time, but you're a good organizer. Things would work out." I tried to encourage her into sharing more of her thoughts.

My husband and I decided to downsize while we still could make our own choices. Since the purchase of our little cruising trawler, Gerald and I enjoyed a carefree lifestyle, ourselves.

Beverly Jane and her husband bought our old home, my Mama's home, where we had raised our family and remodeled it while we were building our "carriage house." I thought of it as a garage makeover, but Beverly Jane insisted on calling it our carriage house.

Lucy continued, "I see Beverly's three children and I love being around them. They are so full of creativity and fun, like when I was growing up. We did have a great time back then, Mama. You and Daddy were, no *are,* terrific parents."

I could smell the chocolate chip cookies baking in the oven and the warm fuzziness of her conversation only added to my bliss. I didn't realize the children were home until I heard the front door slam and tromping on the stairs.

"Did not!"

"Did SO! Oh be quiet, Mullet Head." The younger two of my three neighboring grandchildren hollered at each other.

BEAR WITH ME, DEAR

"It sounds like the 'fun creative little ones' are home," I joked with Lucy.

"Grandma, I need your help." Grace climbed the stairs up to our perch and immediately her voice changed. "Oh, hi Aunt Lucy, I forgot you were here. She turned back to her brother, the middle child. "If you walk the dog today I'll do it *twice* for you when your time comes."

Sweat stuck his hair to his face, Bart or Bartlet, as I call him, brushed aside his bangs. "And take out the garbage this week?" He bargained further with her.

"No way, Turnip Head. Take it or leave it!" Grace stood her ground, hands on her waist, toes pointed straight at her older brother. "That's my final offer."

My poker-playing grandson shrugged, "It was worth a try to up the ante, Turnip Head, yourself. I'll be back, Grandma." He turned and headed for the stairs. "Save some cookies for me, Grandpa!" He dashed over to their house. We could see Maggie Mae, their cockapoo, wagging her tail, greeting him through the screen door. We watched as Bart leashed the dog and went out to the street, plastic poop bag stuck in his back pocket.

Grace plopped down beside me in the glider and swung her legs. "Grandma, I'm just not into history *and* I have a big project *and* I waited too long before I started it *and* well, I need your help or I'm going to make a *D* on it. I have to write about New Bern's twentieth century." With that, she fell back on the bench seat and sighed, very loudly.

Lucy was game with us helping her. She grinned and jumped up and began tickling my youngest grandchild. "No grumpy-grouch, Turnip Head allowed on this bridge, Matey.

BEAR WITH ME, DEAR

Either cheer up and face your responsibilities or we'll toss you overboard!" She pretended to pick Grace up to heave her over the side. Grace screeched, laughed and doubled over to protect her ticklish parts. "Stop! No fair!"

"My mother, your grandmother, just happens to know all about New Bern during the twentieth century. In fact, she lived it!"

I frowned. After all, I didn't come along until it was half over.

"Well, she lived half of it. *AND*, can tell you whatever you need to know, so you are in luck."

Gerri, the oldest of Beverly's children, trotted into view carrying a plate of cookies. "What's going on?" It sounded more like, "Ut's ooing onnnnn?" She had a warm cookie crumbling between her lips. Gerri set the plate down and caught the cookie half before it dropped. "Did she tell you, yet? Logger Head, you need help and Grandma's the only one to do it. Maybe you can drag in Lucy, too."

Lucy and I sat back down to hear the youngest child explain her situation. Gerri hopped up on the porch bench and took off her shoes as Grace struggled with her story.

"OK, just so's you know, I can appreciate you and Mom enjoying your history, but for me, it's boring. I'm just not interested in the history stuff. We were supposed to pick a time in New Bern's history to write a report on and everyone else got the best parts. The Revolutionary War and the Civil War were taken first. I was stuck with the twentieth century. Yucko. Nothing's as boring as that.

"I can't even use Caleb Bradham's invention of Pepsi Cola. That was 1898! I missed out on all the good stuff." She frowned an Emmet Kelly clown face. A tear blossomed in her eye, the poor thing.

"There are lots of things that happened in the 20th century in New Bern. Have you ever heard of the Buggymobile? A man right here in New Bern invented one after seeing an automobile on a trip north. We had the Great Fire of New Bern in 1922. Bayard Wootten was born here and became a nationally known photographer in the early 1900's. She was not only an outstanding artist and photographer, but also, one of our first feminists. She felt strongly about women's rights. After all, she was trespassing in a man's occupation. Her home and studio were right down there on East Front Street. We walked by it many times. You know she designed the first Pepsi Cola logo?" I asked. "You can see what that looks like by visiting Caleb's grave. It's on a stone slab there in Cedar Grove Cemetery.

"Wootten also went up in one of the Wright brothers' first planes and took an aerial photograph of New Bern. No *man* ever thought of doing that until she did. Then we had the two great world wars. New Bern really grew during those times. They even thought German submarines would send spies up the Neuse River." Both she and Gerri frowned, looking down the river.

"Boy Scouts sat in the Courthouse cupola and took turns looking for enemy planes. We also have several ghosts from that period. Did you know we had our own POW camp of Germans whose submarines were sunk off our coast?"

"Huh? You mean we had a prison here in New Bern for the enemy?"

BEAR WITH ME, DEAR

"Yes, right down there close to the river, where we have picnics, at Camp Battle. We now call it Glenburnie Park."

"Can we go see it?"

"Sure, as well as several other places."

Grace pulled a notebook from her book bag and started writing with her purple pen. "You sure know a lot of stuff, Grandma. Can I borrow your brain for a week?" Her grim face began to brighten.

"Why the Palace was rebuilt in New Bern through the efforts of some very hard-working ladies. They fought the government to move the Trent River Bridge and a major highway -- and raised monies to buy up the properties surrounding the Tryon Palace, as you now know it.

"Did you know Elvis Presley was here?

"The real Elvis?" Gerri chimed in with her eyebrows rising into her long red bags. "No way."

"Yep, the real Elvis, not an impersonator. I'm sure you don't know Tyrone Power, but he was a well-known actor and he was stationed here at Cherry Point. He was our version of your Brad Pitt. The girls stood in line to dance with him at the USO.

"What's a USO?"

Lucy said, "It's like a military YMCA for the soldiers in the area, a social club kind of thing."

Grace put her hands on her ears. "Stop, my brain is going to explode, Grandma. It may pop!"

I couldn't resist continuing, "We even had our own sit-ins at the drugstore during integration in the 1960s. *And* talk about scandals, why you could fill a book on all the gossip of murders and men running around with their girlfriends, while their wives looked the other way. So where shall we start?"

"I'd like to hear about the ghosts and running around with girlfriends and not the wives." Gerri raised her eyebrows hopefully.

"Never you mind," I told her. "This is Grace's project."

Gerri snorted, pulled a *Twilight* novel out of her book bag and made herself comfortable, curling up in the corner of the bench.

"Do you have any books I can use as reference? I don't think my teacher will let me say I got all this stuff from my grandma."

The child followed me as I retreated downstairs and pulled several books from the shelves for her to look through. As I was getting her settled, I heard a car pull into the driveway.

Henrietta Geneva Simmons, or Etti G, as we called her, came trotting up to our door. Her red Miata's engine popped as it cooled in our front yard. "Hi, Mrs. Wade, I heard Lucy was in town. Nana says she saw her with you this morning."

She let herself into our front room, without being invited. Her salon-enhanced blonde hair tied into a knot on top of her head allowed several strands to fashionably escape, down the sides of her face. That angel face had way too much makeup on it, as far as I was concerned. Her tongue licked her top lip as she adjusted the bangles on her wrist. The magenta sweater she was wearing barely covered her bellybutton. In addition, the cut-off jeans below that navel had less fabric than my favorite dust cloth!

BEAR WITH ME, DEAR

"Yes, Etti Geneva, we did see your grandmama this morning. She didn't, by any chance, send those brochures with you did she?"

She snapped her fingers. "Golly, I forgot to bring them. My mind is such a mess these days with my wedding coming up pretty soon." She flashed Gerald a sparkling smile. I even caught her winking at him. She waved her left-hand in front of my nose. I couldn't miss the big rock on her ring finger -- or the alcohol breath.

Lucy walked down the steps and stared at her friend from high school.

"Lucy Girl, how long are you in town? We've got so much catching up to do." Etti G ran over and hugged Lucy. Of course, Lucy had to admire her ring. If my memory served me right, that was the third diamond Etti G sported in the past 10 years. This time she was engaged to the lieutenant governor's son, Wellford Dixon Barnes, III, or as we called him, Trey. His daddy, WD Barnes, always walked the middle of the road in politics, but he'd done it successfully since being our local state representative several years before. A flashy man in politics, I'm sure he'd set his cap on the governorship come next election.

"When's the wedding? I'll only be here another week." Lucy turned her head to look at me and rolled her eyes.

"But you can come back, can't you? You don't live that far away. Why, little ole Swansboro's not that far to drive."

Both Lucy and I knew the drive took less than an hour, but it was a long way to come to answer questions and hold hands.

"I really need your help. Nana is about ready to have a fit and Daddy's no help at all.

He's so blasé about my weddings. I need someone like you, steady as a rock, to get me through this."

Always the drama queen, Etti G dropped to her knees and begged Lucy. "Please tell me you'll help. I just love Trey to death. He would do anything for me, too. Come hell or high water, I'm going through with this wedding and marrying that man!

"Daddy wants me to be sure this is the one. Like is it my fault if the other engagements didn't work out? That old battle-axe of a mother my last boyfriend had just about drove me crazy. *BUT*, I just love Mrs. Barnes. She told me she was going to help me as much as I allowed her. She said she always wanted a daughter like me. Isn't she sweet?

"There is no way Nana or Daddy can stop this wedding."

Chapter 3

Lucy pulled her up and assured her she'd help as much as she could. I noticed that Grace absorbed the whole theatrics, forgetting her books to watch her aunt and Etti G. Although the wedding of Trey Barnes and Etti Geneva Simmons might make *history*, this was no concern of Grace's report. I sat down beside her to see how she was getting along.

"I'm going out partying tonight, and you've gotta come with me," Etti G continued.

My internal monitor went on alert. Etti G had liquor on her breath. I certainly didn't want Lucy riding around with her.

Lucy looked back at me before she answered. "What time are you going out? Maybe I can meet you somewhere." What a smart child I had. "Would you like a cup of coffee and just sit here for a while? You can tell

me all about your wedding plans." She held up
her own coffee mug. "You seem all strung out."
That was a polite way of saying, 'You're drunk
as a skunk!'

"Lordy, no, I have things to do and
places to go." She started backing out the door,
as she reached in her purse for her cell phone.
"I'll call you later and tell you what time to meet
us at the Hilton. What's your number? I'll plug
it into my phone." Lucy reeled off our number.
"I'll talk to you later." She let the screen door
slam on her way out.

The red Miata spun on the gravel as she
pulled out of our drive. I cringed when the car's
bottom hit on the street after she peeled out of
the driveway.

Lucy turned to look at me and shirked
her shoulders. "That girl is strung out."

***

Bart and Gerri were both munching on chocolate chip cookies and drinking milk at my kitchen island by the time Beverly Jane, my older daughter, arrived. Grace completed an outline of her 20th century report on New Bern, which I approved. They all followed their mother home.

The house was unusually quiet after an afternoon with my grandkids. Lucy must've noticed it also. "It got quiet all of a sudden, didn't it? I miss not having the kids here." She paused. "Boy, Mama, can you believe Etti G? Drinking has always been one of her problems. Now she drives after she has a drink. I think they let her off too easily the last time. A few days working at the soup kitchen and she thinks she paid her dues. Daddy, if I ever come home swaying like she was, you can tie me to the bedpost until I'm sober."

Gerald replied, "I'd stake you out at low tide and let the crabs have you if you ever came in like that." He was always a *sensitive* man dealing with our children.

She dropped down on the couch beside me. "We were never that bad, were we?"

"All three of you put together were never that bad!" Gerald got up from his recliner to head upstairs for his afternoon siesta. "We had a bit of a problem with Hancock, but he eventually straightened himself out. You girls were no problem, at all. You were my sweeties."

"Oh, Daddy," she leaned over and kissed him. "You are our sugar bear!"

My two girls had twisted their father around their little fingers from the days they were born. I had to put up with all their shenanigans. "Let's pick up those posters from

Etti G's grandmama and get out of here." I whipped off the lap robe and folded it on the couch.

Lucy grabbed her purse. "I'll drive." We both pulled on our jackets and went out to her car. She turned on the radio to a local country classics station. The commercials were already talking about Easter buffets at local restaurants. I reached over and adjusted the volume. She turned her head at me.

"Don't look down your nose at your Mama. That was too loud, girl."

We passed the Pembroke community and headed toward the local Country Club. Olde Towne is one of many communities along the road. Henrietta Gay Simmons moved there after Etti G's mama passed.

"Didn't Etti G's mama die mysteriously or something?"

"I think they said it was an accidental drug overdose. They let it slide. Mr. Simmons is with that big law firm and he wanted to avoid any sensationalism." I filled in what little information I knew.

"Wisely, Ms. Henrietta allowed her son and granddaughter to help her pick out a new home here. Turn here, dear." We made two more turns, according to my directions, before seeing her street numbers.

Brass carriage lamps, like sentinels, led me up the brick, ivy-shouldered walkway. When I pressed the doorbell, I could hear a bell tolling inside. Ms. Henrietta came to the door, herself. I could see all the way through the hallway to the river behind the house.

"Bear with me, dear. I am in such a state! Etti Geneva has run off again, and that son of mine is no help all. If you ask me, his wife took the easy way out with those two!

"Now where did I put those posters and brochures for you?" She led me down a slate-floored hallway and turned into her office. Leather bound books lined one wall. Yellow flowered chintz covered the love seat and matching end chair. Sunny buttery walls trimmed by white crown moldings and spacious windows looked out over the Trent River. It was a lovely setting. A vase of bright orange lilies sat on a Queen Anne side table.

Ms. Henrietta shuffled through a stack of papers and finally found what she was looking for, all the time mumbling to herself. She handed me a stack of posters and brochures. "As you can see, I have a lot on my mind. You had three daughters yourself, didn't you?"

"No, I have two daughters and a son."

"Then you surely must know what I'm going through these days. I've had some horrible news, and I don't know what to do about it." She wrung her well-manicured, but vein-lined hands and shook her head. A piece of long hair fell from the tight bun at her nape. She fingered the lace doily collar as she spoke to me. "But that's not your concern. I wish Peter would have more of a backbone like his daddy. Do you know my son, Peter Simmons? He's an attorney downtown across from the courthouse."

"I've never had the pleasure, no." I responded. "Can I help you with anything else?"

She hesitated, "No, I'll have to deal with it myself, I suppose." She led me back out to the front door. "Oh, before I forget, I'd like you and your daughter to attend one of the functions I'm giving for Etti Geneva."

Her mind immediately switched channels. "Are you familiar with the Questers of New Bern? It's an organization devoted to preserving historical artifacts, memorials, buildings and land sites.

"The local chapter of Questers chose the Cedar Grove Cemetery for its primary project. They offer tours and luncheons to raise money to refurbish the stones and tombs of Cedar Grove.

"At any rate, I'm having such a luncheon at Alice Ruckart's home. I'd like you and Lucy, to be there." She pressed an invitation into my hand.

By the time I returned to the car, Lucy had rolled all the windows down and was fiddling with the radio. "What's up, Mom?"

"Well, I suppose we've been summoned."

"What do you mean, Mama?"

"Ms. Henrietta has requested our attendance at a luncheon she is giving for her granddaughter. We should be honored. I suppose this means we need to go to Belk's to buy a present. What do you give a person who had everything given to her on a silver platter, all her life?"

"Surely she has a gift registry at the department store, Mama. We'll go there after we see this house you've been telling me about. So does Nicholas Sparks live this way?" She pulled back onto the main road.

I directed her along the river until we crossed over Wilson's Creek where we found the house. She pulled into Sparks' driveway to turn around. "Impressive! I'd like to have had that decorating job."

We then went to Belk's and perused Etti G's gift list. Lucy turned up her nose and looked at me. "How many pickle forks does a girl need?"

"Evidently, never enough." We had the forks wrapped and looked for the red dot sale items in the ladies' department.

***

The following Saturday morning I took Beverly's children to the New Bern Fireman's Museum. I figured we could get a visit in before Lucy and I had to go to the luncheon. "Now children, pay attention to what Mrs. Mohr has to say."

Gerri did her frequently visable eye roll; Grace looked hopefully on with pen and tablet held like a prayer book. I had to grab the Bartlett back before he climbed onto a fire wagon. My sweet grandchildren were taxing my patience. Where was Lucy when I needed three hands?

The docent began her tour by leading us over to the various fire alarm systems. "This museum is dedicated to the preservation of two centuries worth of firefighting equipment. The New Bern Fireman's Museum kindles respect for the life-saving missions of Craven County's brave brigade." She then showed us the various horse-drawn fire engines, hose wagons and ladder trucks from the 1800s.

Bart interrupted her, "Do you have any Dalmatians or horses here?"

"Well, we'll get to Fred, our fire horse, in just a minute." Mrs. Morh was one patient woman. "At one time there were competitions among the various fire stations, as to who could get where the fastest with their equipment." She bent over and looked Bart straight in the eye.

Karen Dodd

"Do you know why the firemen had Dalmatian dogs?"

He stared back, but shook his head.

"Their job was to keep other dogs and animals out of the path of the racing horses and fire engine. They have some inbred desire to race in front of the wagons, clearing the way."

"Huh," Bart seemed impressed, but he immediately spied the horse's head encased in a glass box. "Cool!"

"I see you've spied Fred. He died in the line of duty on the way to a fire. His big heart just gave out. If you can wait a minute I'll see if we can't get my old friend to talk to you." The woman's love and knowledge of the fire fighting machinery and its history was evident. She explained how the 1879 Silsby Steam Fire Engine drew up water and pumped it out of the hoses. "When the engineers built streets over our oyster shell roads in the early 1900s, they put in a water system. Up until that time, they had to rely on wells strategically located throughout the town. These two hoses could pump 250 gallons of water per minute."

After the children listened to Fred, the horse, talk about his job, they drifted over to the display cases. Vintage leather fire hats and equipment were enclosed along two walls.

One display detailed the Great Fire of New Bern. Mrs. Mohr continued, "On Friday, December 1, 1922, two fires broke out in New Bern within hours of each other. Although it had been a beautiful, balmy day, wind gusts were recorded at 45 miles per hour. One fire started at the Roland Lumber Company. Another fire started at a private home, when a wash pot blew over. Before the end of the day, 3,000 people were left homeless and $2,000,000 of property was destroyed, but only one life was lost."

"This would've made the evening's national news." I tried to get the children to put the devastation in perspective. "People spent the night camped in the Cedar Grove Cemetery. They had no homes."

When we left the museum, we walked up to see the old fire station on Broad Street. There was a plaque indicating the previous location of the GH Waters' Carriage Company. "This is where the first North Carolina automobile was made. It was called a Buggymobile. The young man who built it used a horse carriage base and put in a one hp motor. He drove it, not with a wheel, but with the tiller." I noted that Gerri was impressed with that information. "When we get home, I'll show you what it looked like." We walked back to the car. As a treat for behaving, I took them to the Cow Café where we all enjoyed ice cream before heading home.

Gilbert S. Water's Buggymobile in New Bern (Credit and thanks to the NC Business History website)

Chapter 4

I drove to the luncheon, while Lucy navigated. "According to the address on this, it should be at the next corner, Mama." She held our gift in her lap and the invitation rested on top with her purse.

The home was on the corner of Johnson and Craven Streets. When we arrived, Alice Ruckart invited us into her living room. The beautiful home, restored by the couple, was open to the public when she hosted the Quester luncheons. I was surprised to hear Ms. Henrietta and Etti G arguing in the hall.

"You will not do any such thing!"

"I don't care what you think, Nana, my mind is made up."

They had the good grace to stop quarreling when we entered the living room.

"Fiona, I'm so glad you and your lovely daughter could come today." Miss Henrietta poured on the charm. "Etti Geneva, why don't you and your friend, Lucy, sit over there. We'll take these chairs." She sat erect, her legs properly crossed at her ankles. "Have you had a busy week, dear?" She addressed Lucy, "I understand you will only be here a few more days."

"Yes ma'am." Lucy answered, "While my husband is out of town on business, I thought I'd visit Mama. We've revisited all the wonderful places in town that the tourists usually come and see." She turned to our hostess. "I understand you also lead tours of the Cedar Grove Cemetery. I think that would be fun." She turned to me, "Mama, have you ever gone on a Quester tour?"

"We'll have to find out more about it," I said. "Of course I've gone on the Ghostwalks they do every October." Ghostwalks in New Bern are a yearly event. Sponsored by the Historical Society, scripts are written by local historians for actors to play at various homes and locations throughout town. Horse drawn carriages, trolley rides and various churches join in the fun, providing meals and entertainment for the All Saints' activities.

Within the half hour, all eight guests arrived. We lunched on hot chicken salad, homemade biscuits, asparagus, a gelatin molded to perfection and hot tea. It was delicious. After eating, the girls gathered to watch Etti Geneva open her presents, sometimes shrieking in surprise, while the rest of us oohed and aahed.

I left the young women to find our luncheon hostess looking on from the hallway. "Tell me more about these Questers."

BEAR WITH ME, DEAR

Mrs. Ruckart said, "You know we are part of the international organization founded in 1944. Well, our 20 members live in the historic district of town. Our Questers Chapter started 14 years ago in New Bern. We are not as much into collecting, but we promote the preservation and restoration of all things historical. We also provide scholarships to Columbia University students interested in historical architecture and archaeology." She glanced into her living room to see if anyone needed anything. Other Questers were handling the clearing of the table and serving more tea and pecan tarts for dessert. I declined, having had ice cream before the luncheon.

"Our main project is Cedar Grove Cemetery. We meet on a regular basis to discuss our business, plan luncheons like these, and give guided tours of the cemetery each Saturday evening."

"I had no idea you existed."

"Well, we aren't allowed to use money to advertise and the New Bern Historical Society helps by giving out our brochures. We try to let people know about our tours. So far, we raised over $30,000. We've repaired masonry, made minor preservation on a triage basis, completing the worst things first at the cemetery. Some of the old tombs had falling roofs and crumbling walls. We had to restore them because there were no families to provide for their upkeep. When we find no surviving family members who can help financially, we often undertake such a project."

"I never knew about you." I was amazed at their dedication. "I'd like to take your graveyard stroll. You say every Saturday. What time?" She told me that with spring's arrival, the new scheduling of guided tours began again. I made a mental note of the times.

BEAR WITH ME, DEAR

Lucy stuck her head into the hallway. "Mama, things are winding up. Are you about ready to leave?"

I went to look for my purse and shawl. After saying thanks to the two hostesses, Etti G and Ms. Henrietta, we left.

Chapter 5

When we got home, I had a message to call my cousin Boo, or Buford Waters. I've called her Boo ever since we were little girls. She recently bought a condominium at SkySail, downtown just a few blocks from where we live.

"You called?" I said.

"I haven't seen you since New Year's Eve. I'll take most of the blame since I've been busy moving and decorating for the past three months. You care to go for a walk? I need to get out of here for a while, and it's such a pretty day."

I looked at my watch. It read past two. "Lucy is here visiting. If I can get the grandchildren to come, we will look like a gaggle of geese crossing the street. Give us 15 minutes to change, and we will meet you at the corner of South Front and East Front Streets." I hung up the telephone. Then I called Grace. I wanted her to see Bayard Wootten's house. "Bring your camera, Sugar. This will be good for your report."

By the time we were changed, Beverly Jane, Gerri, Grace and Bart had joined our walking group. We straggled down to the corner meeting Boo as she crossed in front of the Convention Center.

She hugged everyone, making comments as she went from person to person. "Goodness gracious, you children grow up so fast. Gerri, you're a teenager now! I think you've grown three inches since the last time I saw you. Grace, what a good-looking young lady you have become and Bart, you look like your daddy, all handsome and grown-up. What are you 10-11? Beverly Jane, you certainly have a fine looking family." She then turned to Lucy,

"And you look mighty fine too, even without a flock of children."

Lucy shrugged. I was the only one who noticed a bit of sadness on her face. I wondered if she was still thinking about her potential child.

It continued to be a gorgeous day. I held Grace's camera, while she and the others raced along the riverfront walk. We three grownups followed at a more leisurely pace, reading plaques implanted along the walk. A flock of pigeons took off as the children neared.

We rounded the Comfort Inn, walked past Persimmon's Restaurant and approached the old bridge cutoff. Several people were fishing from the edge of the walkway.

"And Boo, tell us about your condo. Mother mentioned you had moved. What floor are you living on? Can you see both rivers?"

BEAR WITH ME, DEAR

Beverly Jane was actually taking an interest in someone else for a change.

"You must come see it. I'm so proud of myself. Most of my furniture worked fine with the layout of the unit. Yes, I can see both rivers and my patio opens to the west. So I can see sunsets every day." Boo beamed with pleasure talking about her new home.

"Lucy, I wish I had your color sense to help me when I painted the living room and bedroom. Maybe you can give me some pointers if you come by." Boo tied her cardigan sweater around her neck. I always admired the way she put her clothes together. Even her walking shoes were a designer's match to her aquamarine jogging suit. She had applied makeup, also, before coming. Mine was fading fast from our luncheon.

Bart said, "Look at all the fish he's caught! Wow, maybe Daddy can bring us back and we can go fishing some day."

Beverly Jane's eyebrows went up as she peered into the bucket. "Perhaps someday we can. We'll have to ask your father." Beverly Jane was also dressed up. I've never seen this child in a pair of jeans, well, not since she was 16. A pale rose sweater and khaki slacks, complete with Bass Weejuns - her idea of casual attire.

Lucy wore a flannel shirt, neatly tucked into her faded jeans and thick socks peeled down over the tops of her Doc Martens. A pale lip-gloss was her only makeup. She had scrubbed her face clean after the luncheon. How did I rear two such different girls?

The children continued to lope along in front of us as we quickened our pace. Bart had raced ahead and found the Bayard Wootten historical plaque.

Grace asked, "So, she lived here? With her two children and her mother? Where was her studio?"

"It burned down years ago. She had another studio in town, but she finally moved to Chapel Hill. You read where she was in New York City for a while." I crossed the street and called Grace over so she could take a picture. Afterwards, Grace copied everything down that was on the historical marker.

Beverly Jane suggested, "Why don't we walk on over to the Bank of the Arts. They're supposed to have a display there this week of all Wootten's work. UNC at Chapel Hill has loaned the photographs."

Karen Dodd

Bayard Wootten's Home

Chapter 6

The former bank building is now headquarters for the Cravens Arts Council and Gallery. Built in 1913, it was judicially restored recently to house both musical and visual arts events monthly. There's no fee for visiting. Gerald and I visit at least once a month to see the featured artists.

"Hey everybody, let's go this way." Lucy redirected the children down Johnson Street back towards Middle Street.

"Can we go to the Cow Café afterwards? Please. I love going there." Grace asked.

"Sure, my treat," Boo answered. "There's some social event going on there today. It should be fun."

Karen Dodd

House Number 1

The Bank of the Arts was packed. I noticed the Lt. Governor and his staff were present, as well as several other local politicians. People stood in line to shake hands.

The display was outstanding. Bayard Wootten's prints filled the entire gallery atrium. I was lost in admiration and my own reflections when two voices interrupted my thoughts. The conversation was coming from the inside the bank vault, a small intimate room off the atrium.

"We've got to do something about her, Dixon. If anyone *else* finds out about what we've been doing, you can kiss your job goodbye."

"Job! Hell, we'd go to jail, WD." Their voices shifted to whispers as they walked into the main gallery. I shrank behind the vault door, as they passed.

Let me explain what our Bank of Arts looks like. You walk between two impressive double doors, passing through tall Corinthian columns. A two-story chamber is the main gallery. You can go to the store in the back either of two ways. One is a narrow hallway of paintings and sculptures; the other is through the bank vault. It opens into the combination office and store where you can buy prints, paintings, woven art, jewelry and various artists' products. The vault also contains a display of more items for sale. The heavy door, complete with tumblers and locks, opens into the gallery.

I was admiring the prints behind the vault door, when I heard the men's exchange. I know they didn't notice me when they left.

I found Boo buying a pair of earrings at the cash register. "Did you just hear that? A man called Dixon and our Lt. Gov. Barnes were talking inside the vault."

"No, Honey, there's so many people in here I'm surprised you could hear anything. Was it important?"

"I rather think it was." I grabbed her arm and pulled her back to the vault to see where the men were. They walked out the front door and stopped abruptly. Henrietta Simmons was waiting for them. "Come on, I want to see what happens." I called to my daughters as I passed. "Beverly Jane, Lucy, we'll meet you and the children at the Cow Café in a few minutes."

We pushed our way through the gathering, but by the time we passed through the front door, the two men and Ms. Henrietta were gone.

Boo confronted me. "Well, what on earth was so important that we had to rush out here?" She stood there with her mouth open. Her latest purchase dangled from one hand.

I told her about the conversation I overheard. "What else did they say? Do you know who or what they were talking about? You think Ms. Henrietta was there to ambush them? Fiona, sometimes I think your mind makes up predicaments just so you can complicate matters and cause the lot of us to worry about you! Don't do this again. There are no mysteries for you to solve. They could've been talking about anything. Men always exaggerate. Nothing could be as sinister as you suppose." She tucked her package under her arm and said, "Forget it. Let's go get some ice cream. I want something cool on the back of my throat. You know we walked a long ways."

"Maybe you're right. It was probably nothing." I lied. "I think I'll order moonilla this afternoon. You know this is the second time I've come here today. I brought the children here earlier this morning after we visited the Fireman's Museum."

"You're such a softy. Come on."

Beverly Jane, Lucy and the children waited in line as we pushed our way into the storefront. A miniature train circled the track over our heads as we ordered. Cows stared and glared at us from every angle - furry cows, plastic cows, paper cows, cloth cows, all kinds of cows except real ones are for sale in this café, with all cow-type accoutrements.

The Cow Café, originally located at the Maola Milk Plant, in Riverside, moved downtown, when the milk plant sold to a larger conglomerate.

The Cow Café on Middle Street is a favorite stop for young families with children. The place was jammed with people, baby strollers and high chairs. The smell of roasted hot dogs and popcorn filled the air. We took our purchases of homemade ice cream and went outside to sit at the tables along the front of the café.

"So, Grace, did you take good notes of all that? I bet you found more about Bayard Wootten than you want to know." Lucy took a lick off her double scoop of Mooberry Mousse ice cream cone, raspberry swirls and chocolate chunks. "Did you have any idea when you started this project all the things we'd do?" She took another lick. "Grandma and I are going to visit the graveyard. Is anyone up for that next Saturday?"

"I have an auxiliary meeting next Saturday, but the children can go." Beverly sucked up a mouthful of her chocowlate shake and daintily wiped her lips with a paper napkin. She looked at her ice cream-faced children. "You want to go the cemetery with Grandma next week?"

Lucy counted sticky hands raised in the air. "It's not that far. We'll make it a hike and pack a picnic. I bet we can find a place to sit and eat sandwiches."

"Can we make pimento cheese and pickle sandwiches?" Bart always had to be different.

"Pimento Head!" Gerri rebuffed her brother. "I want a BLT."

"BLT Head, I'll make a PB&J for me." Lucy laughed a she contributed her alphabet menu item.

"Mom, can I make a PB&J&M&M sandwich?" Grace with chocolate smears on her cheeks giggled at her mother. Grace was my most creative grandchild.

"I think not," Beverly replied. "But you can each take a package of candy for dessert. I'll contribute a jug of lemonade, too."

Boo added, "Am I included? I'll make my world famous brownies if you let me come."

Gerri nudged her elbow, as her eyebrows bobbed, "You are so in, Cousin Boo!"

"Say, I almost forgot. Grandpa said we could all go out on the boat next Saturday." I added to the melee of plans.

"Great and I'm going to drive!" Bart said.

"Young man, don't you have a fife and drum performance that afternoon? Mother, will you be back in time?"

Trent River Tree

"We are only going up the Trent River and back." I lowered my voice. "I hear there is a dead man waving from the top of a tree on the Trent. Do you want to go see him?"

Grace chimed in, "I *must* take a picture of that."

Gerri scoffed, "There's no such thing."

"Oh yes, there is," said Boo.

Bart said it all, "Awesome."

Chapter 7

"Mom, this has been fun." Lucy and I drove up to Riverside with Boo on Monday evening to walk. "It's been a combination old home week and vacation for me. I felt like a tourist, visiting all the tourist attractions of New Bern."

"Did you get by the Academy?" Boo asked. "I hear they changed the exhibits and I want to see them."

"Yes, we did, Boo. They have a Civil War display and of course, the school's history, but I love studying all the New Bern architecture. There is a whole floor dedicated to that!"

"Look at that house. Someone really loves it to do all that work." I stopped to admire the new re-work in progress.

BEAR WITH ME, DEAR

House Number 2

"That's one of the best things about this town, the way home owners appreciate and restore what we have here instead of tearing it all down like they did in downtown Morehead City."

Large hardwood trees, with leaves in a variety of greens, hung over our heads. The root systems buckled the sidewalks out of place. Moss crept from cracks in the shadows, forming thick spider webs in the old concrete. The ripening of spring's earth and budding filled the air. We walked to the stop light at the end of the residence walk and turned, returning to Boo's car.

"Want to come in for dinner, Boo?"

"And eat up all those pounds I lose by the walking? No, thank you. Besides, there is a program at the library tonight. Sid Livingston asked me to go with him." We got out of her Big Red Cadillac. "It's a program on the "Queen Anne's Revenge" they are excavating off the coast near Beaufort. Sounds like a cheap date to me, but we may stop and get a sandwich afterwards." She waved before backing out of the driveway.

Lucy and I could smell the barbecued ribs before we walked through the door. "Oh, Daddy, you cooked ribs!" Lucy skipped over to her father and hugged the man.

Gerald beamed, "I don't get to cook for my baby very often. We are so glad you decided to come and visit with us."

"I'm not your baby anymore, Daddy." She pursed her lips and acted as if she was going to say something else, but didn't. "Mama, what can I do to help?"

"Set the table dear and I'll make us all a drink or would you rather have wine?"

"I don't feel like wine, but I'd love a tall glass of sweet tea, Mama. You know I saw Etti G again today." She hung our jackets on the wall rack and turned. "I think she had a beer before she came to the Y. How can she keep doing that with alcohol and driving?"

Gerald responded, "I don't know, but she is going to do something terrible. Mark my words."

I heated the twice-baked potatoes and Lucy finished making the salads. The ribs were delicious, but messy. We were loading the dishwasher when Lucy answered the phone.

"Oh, hi, Etti G? What you up to?" She looked at her watch. "Golly, I'm sorry. I already have plans. Maybe I can meet you for breakfast tomorrow morning. I'm dying for some Baker's Square French toast. Wanna come meet me around nine in the morning?" She paused. "Well, that's sorta late. How about 9:30? You can surely make it by then, can't you?" She paused to listen. "I don't care if you don't put on all your makeup before breakfast, silly." She took the sponge and wiped off the kitchen counter as she listened. "Well, I gotta go now. I'll talk with you in the morning. I'll see you at 9:30 then. Bye."

Baker's Square is a restaurant owned by Mennonites who live in the area. All their food is prepared using their recipes. Their breads and pastries rival my own. However, their French toast and syrupy topping, I can't make. It's our family 'special occasion' breakfast to eat there some mornings.

She turned to me as I finished the baking dish pre-scrub, turned it upside down in the dish rack and shut the dishwasher door. "I'm awful, but I just don't want to go out and 'party' with her. I think she's partied enough and it's time to grow up. Do you think she'll settle down once she and Trey marry?"

Gerald relaxed into his recliner and folded the paper for his crossword puzzle. "Well, time will tell, don't you think? But boy, I pity the man who has to tame that young'un."

***

The next morning, Lucy pulled on a teal blue sweater over her jeans and dashed off to meet her friend for breakfast. I ate my whole-wheat toast and fig preserves, while Gerald prepared to meet his coffee klatch friends.

"I hear that Marissa and Mack will be home sometime this month." He knew I was anxious to see my friend and hear about their live-aboard journey up from Beaufort and Charleston, SC. "I guess he's glad he bought that larger sailboat last year."

I had read their log entries on Facebook. "The last time I heard from them they were in Wrightsville Beach, anchored out. They sent a notice from a local coffee shop. It appeared that there is always somewhere with wireless connections that boaters and travelers can use." I smiled a smug grin at my spouse. "I knew they'd hit it off from the beginning."

I introduced the couple the previous fall and was delighted they enjoyed each other's company enough to make a commitment. Gerald and I signed their marriage license shortly after New Year's Day. The small ceremony, held in her family home, united a rough-cut live-aboard and a jewel of a friend. I was very happy for them.

The couple left late on their southern journey after I discovered who killed Maynard Battle, a local politician. Marissa had been arrested for his murder, but that's another story.

"I'll be back around 11 this morning. You have any plans?" Gerald put his Outer Banks baseball cap on his head and reached for his windbreaker.

"We'll be here when you get back." I finished my breakfast and went upstairs to brush my teeth, then sat and knitted in the morning sun on our deck.

Lucy returned home, miffed. "Wanna go for a walk Mama?" She threw her purse down on the deck and walked over to where I was sipping lukewarm coffee "She came late and she was hung over. I am so mad, I could chew nails."

"Let me put on my shoes and we'll walk off your frustration." Lucy changed into her own pair of walking shoes and pulled on a sweatshirt. "Thanks, Mama."

This time we headed south around the convention center and then turned west along the waterfront. Spring was in the air. More boats were in the marina as some of the early snowbirds were heading north. "Let's go down and check the lines on our boat and then we can follow the shore line," I suggested.

The Hilton Marina faces south, between the Trent River Bridge and the railroad bridge.

BEAR WITH ME, DEAR

Huge Hatteras yachts, sailboats, powerboats, locals and travelers rent space. Travelers like the location because the town is within walking distance.

House Number 3

Across the river, the Bridgepoint Marina reaches out to the Hilton, like two opposing thumbs pointing at the bridge. Boats, sheltered from storms, hunker down in their slips and gently rock, having only wind tide and few wakes to disturb them. We keep our own 25-foot Rosborough trawler docked there. We bought it last Christmas and have enjoyed cruising more than once during the warmer days of the winter months.

"She looks fine, Mom."

I checked the dock lines and adjusted a fender. "You're right. It's just that she's like a new baby to us. I have to keep fussing over her."

"Is it me or am I super sensitive when the word 'baby' is used?" She was gnawing on her lip again, a sure sign that something bothered her.

"I'm sorry. I hadn't realized it affected you so. Is everything ok with you and Sam?"

"Of course, everything is fine!" We climbed off the floating dock and turned to walk the sidewalk west along the town's waterfront.

"I don't know if I want to be a mother. I don't know if I'm cut out for it."

"Hush, I've seen you with Beverly's children. I know you have a heart big enough to make the right decisions and love a child. Any child would be special having you as a mother." I hugged her close.

"I'm thinking about the mess Etti G has made of her life. She's so unhappy and yet so rich!"

"You are not Etti G's fairy godmother. You can't fix her, sweetie."

"Uh-huh. I can't believe the state she was in when she got there. I ordered and ate before she arrived. I ordered another refill as she drank coffee and watched me. She could hardly put two words together and make any sense. She didn't eat. Do you think it's only the upcoming wedding? I remember being very nervous about mine."

I reached out and took her hand. "You were nervous as any bride, but certainly not as bad as Etti G. Let's try to forget her and her problems. Enjoy our walk. How about I treat you to a ticket into our new NC History Museum at Tryon Palace? It recently opened during the 300th birthday celebration of New Bern. Let's take a look-see when we get there." We walked further along the waterfront path and stopped at the dock in the back of the Museum.

"It's beautiful."

"Come on, I want to show you the interior. Remember when Barbour Boat Works was here?"

NC History Museum from the Trent River

"They made beautiful wooden cruisers for a while, didn't they?"

"Yes, but during the war they built net tenders, mine sweepers and salvage ships for our government and Great Britain." I led her up to the door and we entered the large atrium. A gift shop and café were located down one hall. Other halls led to exhibits and the children's hands-on activities at the Pepsi exhibition with its latest interactive technology. Children and adults are fascinated with the mix of history and science. There was a brass ensemble practicing on the stage of the concert auditorium.

We turned and stood at the door. "The vaulted ceiling of this area was inspired by the Barbour boat shed that stood here during the 1900's. Isn't it magnificent?"

"It's all quite impressive. I find it hard to believe this is all in New Bern." We wandered through some of the free exhibits depicting New Bern's history and viewed a movie about the earlier times of coastal North Carolina. Then we left the hall and walked up to Pollock Street and past the Tryon Palace.

"Isn't this where you found that dead man last year?" Lucy pointed to a house on the corner.

BEAR WITH ME, DEAR

Atrium of the NC History Museum at Tryon Palace

"Yes, but let's turn up this way and walk back toward home." I didn't want to think about the two dead bodies I encountered last year. "I'm through finding bodies, and, better still, solving murders." I shivered, thinking about it. "Sometimes, I think bodies find me and not the other way around."

"Well, I'll make sure we don't find any on the way home, ok?" Lucy tucked her hand into my elbow and we continued up the street.

"I'm feeling better already. Ole Etti G sure put me into a funk. I don't know why I let her do that." Lucy rubbed her arms, crossing her hands across her chest. "She went on and on about this big truck that Trey bought and how they argued last night. He didn't want her driving it. I'm sure he knows her drinking can do more than wreck a big truck."

"She's hurting and wants to dump on you, dear. You have such a kind heart."

"It's a stupid, big red truck, for goodness sakes. Of all the things to argue about with the man she is about to marry!"

***

On Tuesday, we went to Morehead City to eat seafood and toured Beaufort. Beaufort is another North Carolina town founded on the water in the 1700's. It has been invaded by pirates, ghosts and Union forces, but now by tourists and history buffs, like New Bern. Both towns enjoy the tourists that come for the history, beautiful old homes and waterfront walks.

Gerald took his usual place on the boardwalk. "I'll be here when you two finish shopping." He strolled away looking at the boats docked or moored in Taylor's Creek.

By chance, we met a cousin, Quinn Winslow. She retired to Morehead City after working many years in Raleigh and refurbished an old house herself. "Why, Quinn, what a nice surprise!"

"Fiona," she hugged Lucy and me. "Look at you. Lucy, you are a young woman now. How time flies." She turned back to me, "How many grandchildren do you have now, three, four?"

I nodded.

She didn't wait for an answer. "Lucy, did you contribute to all those grandchildren?"

Lucy shrugged, "Not yet. We are -- thinking about it."

"Well, take your time, hon. I want you to meet a friend of mine. Now where did Charles go?" She glanced about. "He's looking at the boats probably. That's what men do. By the way, where is Gerald?"

I answered, "Probably the same place your Charles is." We walked between stores and browsed the end of winter sales racks. We found both our men and stopped for a cup of coffee at a waterfront pub.

Quinn introduced us to the tall man, Charles, who looked as if he were a retired Marine. The man touched his hand to his floppy brimmed hat and sat at parade rest as we talked.

BEAR WITH ME, DEAR

"Come see us in New Bern. You know, we sold Mama's house and built us a little retirement cottage behind it. Beverly Jane, my oldest, bought the big house."

"I heard that from someone. Your home was next to my Aunt Grace's home. I remember going there as a girl. Yes, I'd love to see what you've done."

Both men trailed us as we walked down the other side of the street. As we ducked in and out of shops, we caught up with each other's family news.

We ate lunch at the Beaufort Grocery Company, making plans for their New Bern visit.

Charles said, "Gerald tells me you also bought a little cruising boat. I'd like to see that. I'm thinking along the same lines."

"Oh, wouldn't that be fun, to cruise somewhere together on our boats!"

"Are y'all ever going to grow up and act your age?" Lucy joked with us.

"Lord, I hope not." We said our goodbyes. Gerald tucked us into our car and drove home to New Bern.

House Number 4

Chapter 8

"Look, look, I see him! Grandpa, move the boat closer so I can take a picture." Grace danced along the stern of the boat as we all stared at the skeleton waving from the top of the tree."

Bart started making boy noises, a cross between spooky howls and yodeling goatherds. "Whoooooooo."

"OK, we've found him. It's not real is it?" Practical Gerri wasn't having anything to do with the spoof. "I mean someone just stuck him up there, didn't they?" She looked at the top of the tree. "Where do you buy life sized plastic skeletons?"

Boo said, "He looks real enough to me. This is as close as I want to get."

We'd been on the river all morning, cruising along one side and then coming back along the other.

Boo looked at her watch. "Bart, what time do we need to get you home?"

"Awww, I never get to have fun. Why can't I stay with y'all?"

I told him, "Because you have responsibilities and a program to get to. Captain, turn this ship toward the dock."

Gerald saluted me, "The admiral speaks and we jump, lad." Gerald allowed the frowning boy to guide the boat back under the Trent River high-rise bridge and then through the railroad bridge. After we fed Bart his pimento cheese sandwich with pickles, Gerald declined our hike invitation and drove Bart to his fife and drum meeting. We slapped sandwiches together and filled the thermos with lemonade.

House Number 5

I'd bought a wheeled carrier for laundry
and supplies for when we live aboard our boat.
It served that day as an excellent carrier for our
evening hike and dinner at Cedar Grove
Cemetery. A few of the crepe myrtle trees along
the way were still in winter drag, branches like
spooky fingers grabbed for the sky.

"Why do some of the crepe myrtles look
like angry fists and others are like long fingers
in lace?" Lucy studied the two sides of the
street where both kinds waved at each other.

I said, "I hate when they cut them back like that. It's all knuckles when they trim them. They should at least cut them in a different place each year so they don't grow like that."

Boo added, "I never cut crepe myrtles back and they were fine at the old house."

Grace and Gerri sang witchy songs they remembered from Halloween. The girls pulled our little cart of goodies, bouncing between cracks and up and down curbs. Boo's clothes matched ours. Only a fuchsia scarf showed at her neck on her otherwise black velveteen jumpsuit.

Lucy and I followed along completing the coven of witches, minus a couple of members, in our dark nylon windbreakers and jeans. A cool breeze blew out of the north, adding eeriness to the angry-looking trees and our mood.

House Number 6

As we neared the graveyard, the girls got the sillies. "Did they put all this Spanish moss up for us and the tour or is it always here?"

"Oh, look at those little houses. They look like Snoopy's doghouse! What if we crawl up on them and pretended to be Snoopy sleeping on top?"

"Hush girls, behave now. Those are gravehouses. People are buried in them." Lucy reprimanded them, which quieted them for a moment.

"Oooooh, spooky Snoopy doghouses!" Then Gerri spied a funny dressed man creeping among the trees toward our party. "Look, what do you suppose he is?"

"Hush, behave and maybe you'll find out." Lucy grabbed the cart from the girls and pulled it toward the arch.

As promised, the Questers stationed at the marl archway that evening handed out brochures. We introduced ourselves to the group already gathered. The guides led us down the shell path into the main part of the cemetery. Highlights included the graves of several state congressmen, judges and our own Caleb Bradham, with Pepsi Cola scripted across his gravestone.

BEAR WITH ME, DEAR

The spirit of former statesman and dualist, John Stanly, made an appearance. He showed us his family plot and mentioned how disappointed he was of the state of his marble gravestone. He was the quaintly dressed re-enactor creeping among the tombstones the children saw. "I haven't been buried 200 years yet and look how it looks! This is preposterous." He showed us the crumbling brownstone in the next plot and said his marker cost many times more than the other did. "I can't believe the scoundrels who sold me this bill of goods, longer lasting marble, ha! The joke is on me and I can't do a wretched thing about it. See how discolored my grave marker is. You cannot even read the inscription. I told them what to put there." He touched the engraved words with his fingers and then rambled off saying he had other family he wished to visit.

Gracie shivered and said, "He gave me the heebie- geebies."

"He was only an actor, Ghostbuster-Goober. Come on." Gerri punched her little sister on the shoulder and then followed Mrs. Mansfield, our guide, further into the graveyard.

Fountain at Cedar Grove

We stopped at Captain William Willis Roberts' grave. "Captain Roberts accompanied Admiral Perry when he sailed into Japan to open trade negotiations for our country. Captain Roberts remembered how the ladies of his family loved gardening, so on his return, he brought a sack with several bulbs in it from Japan. The spider lily bulbs had never been grown in this country." The Quester pointed to the blades of green surrounding the new gravestone. "These will bloom in the fall. You can now find spider lilies all over this country and especially here in New Bern. In fact, the 30-foot kinetic statue behind the convention center on Riverwalk represents Captain Robert's gift of lilies. Have you seen it?'

Some of the group had seen it when they visited the Convention Center. I promised the girls we'd walk down and look at it.

Another marker of interest was the tomb of Confederate soldiers. "The women who buried these men wanted them to be buried with dignity and in full uniform." A tall monument of a Confederate soldier looking south stood in the middle of the large underground vault. "There are about 70 bodies beneath this ground. Not long ago, grave robbers broke in and stole things like belt buckles, insignia and parts of the uniforms. Since then we have sealed the tomb. More soldiers died from disease during the Civil War than from bullets."

We continued the walk around the gravesites. "The restoration of this fountain was one of our major projects. The city has no funds to maintain this entire site except to cut the grass. They provide the manpower to complete some of the work. Our objectives are to preserve and restore this entire site. The money you paid for this tour finances the restoration and preservation of various stones and monuments here."

We returned to the marl archway. "These walls were put up to keep livestock out of the cemetery. This used to be the countryside and animals roamed freely here. Their ramblings through the gravesites knocked over monuments and caused a great deal of damage."

The tour guide stood for a minute and put a hand to her ear. "Did you hear that? It sounded like a bell, didn't it?"

No one else heard it. She shook her head and softly laughed. "Ever hear the expression, dead ringer? At one time, we buried people before they died, by accident, of course. With some illnesses, a person often went into a coma. Some survived their coma, but had no way of calling for help from the closed coffin. Therefore, the survivors put bells in the coffins in case someone woke up. Hear it?" She stopped again and then smiled as both Gerri and Grace strained their ears. "No, I guess not. Sorry, I must be mistaken. Now you know how the term dead ringer came into being." She smiled at us.

At the conclusion of the tour, the Quester suggested we spread our meal on a stone table that looked like it erupted from a mausoleum.

"That wasn't so bad." Gerri swallowed her last bite of banana and peanut butter sandwich. It was sorta interesting." She popped an M&M into her mouth. "So Doodle Head, have you got enough information for your report yet?"

"You're the big Doodle Head, yourself!" She tossed a candy in the air and caught it in her mouth. "I think so. Grandma, just off the top of your head can you think of anything else that happened in the last century?"

BEAR WITH ME, DEAR

Cedar Grove's 6-pointed star also found in Christian symbolism

"Well, did you know our town's four-sided clock tower was the first of its kind in the state, if not the world? I'll have to look up and see when it was added to the town hall. New Bern was also the first town in North Carolina to decorate for Christmas with colored lights. That had to be the last century. We also built the first movie picture theater, from the ground up. Before that, they used old show stages. Hmmm. You have everything else. We better check the dates though."

Grace diligently wrote all this down in her little spiral notebook. "I'll check it out at the library, thanks." After our meal, Grace took pictures as Lucy taught Gerri how to make rubbings on a few stone markers.

We packed away our trash, but a baggy blew out of my hand. It skipped down a line of headstones. Every time I bent to retrieve it, another gust of wind lifted it further into the graveyard.

I regretted the fact that we didn't drive, as I trailed the taunting baggy further into the headstone maze. The temperature was dropping, but I figured a brisk walk home would keep us warm. "Gotcha!" I pressed my foot down on the errant plastic bag. When I picked it up, something white lay crumpled on the ground. "Why it's a piece of lace? What in the world?"

BEAR WITH ME, DEAR

Boo bobbed up behind me. "Before I forget, I wanted to ask you - say what?" We stood halfway down a roadside wall further in the back of the cemetery. "What did you find?" She leaned in to see it.

"Well, if I didn't know better, I'd say it was an old lace collar, you know the kind Ms. Henrietta wears." I straightened up and looked over Boo's shoulder. "Oh, no."

There she lay facing her maker, on a crumbling stone table monument, hands crossed over her chest, paisley print dress wilting in the evening mist. There was no doubt in my mind. She was dead.

"Goodness gracious!" Boo followed my line of vision. "Surely she's sleeping or -- she isn't real, is she?" She clasped her own hands. "You touch her or quick, tell me this is a bad prank teenagers have played."

"I'm afraid not. Here, I have my cell phone. While I call the police, you go back and tell the Questers what we found. Then take the children home. Lucy will help you. I don't want them seeing her like this."

One of the Questers came and stood with me while the other ushered the children out to the gate and waited for the police. I could see the police station from where I stood, but it seemed like forever before I saw a pair of uniformed men walking across the street and up to the gated archway. I pulled my jacket closer to my body and shuffled towards them.

"Have the kids been up to their tricks again. Mrs. Wade? This graveyard gets all kinds of pranks during the year, especially the Ghostwalk weekends in the fall."

I directed the two officers along the dwindling driveway and then turned them to see what I knew was there, hiding behind a crumbling mausoleum. "Look around there."

The officer continued his tale, "Why I remember…." He stopped, stood very still, slowly moving his head from side to side, taking in the body on the slab and all the surroundings.

"Tell me, is this the way you found her? Anyone else around?"

I told him we had been on a tour and stayed to make rubbings and eat our sandwiches.

He reached for his walkie-talkie and called in some information. The number sequences he spoke confounded me. I'll never understand how they can reduce life's cruelties into a series of numbers recited repeatedly on a radio during police protocol.

Soon a medical examiner and crime scene team arrived. They asked me the same questions, again. I thought I would be more believable if an old friend was there. "Is Detective Ron Meadows around? Ron has worked on a couple of prior cases with me."

"No ma'am, he's not working this evening."

Peter Simmons, Miss Henrietta's son, arrived to identify the body. A thin man, he stood looking down at what was left of his mother, shaking his head. His suit and tie appeared fresh, as if he stopped at home and changed before coming. The starched long-sleeved shirtsleeves stuck out of each sleeve as if he measured each cuff for appearances sake. His close-cropped head bowed for a moment.

He looked around as if he expected a judge to appear and dismiss everyone, but no robed court arbiter materialized. Instead, a solemn medical examiner arrived and carted off Ms. Henrietta's remains for autopsy.

"Did you see what happened to her?" Like a child, not the solicitor he presented in court, his empty gaze focused on me. His hand brushed his forehead.

"No, I'm sorry. I don't know how - " There was no question in my mind. His mother was dead and her body was as cold as the marble slab on which she lay.

A uniformed officer drove me home.

I can only say that Gerald, my Dear Husband, put his arms around me when I arrived. I could tell he was agitated about this new discovery, but he held his thoughts as he comforted me.

Chapter 9

Lucy was visibly upset, "Mama, how do you do this?"

"What? I did nothing," I clarified. Gerald was listening when I said, "I found her, but Boo was with me, too. It's not like an Easter egg hunt when you'd go searching for a body under a bush!"

Gerald shook his head and went to the kitchen to make a fresh pot of coffee. "Come sit down. I can see you're upset about this. Boo left some brownies for you."

"I'm sorry, Mother." Lucy sat on the couch sucking at the inside of her cheek. "Poor Etti G, I guess her wedding will have to be delayed. There may not be a wedding anyway, unless they made up today." Lucy took her cell phone out onto the porch. I heard her calling her husband.

BEAR WITH ME, DEAR

The next morning's newspaper headlines told about the murder of Henrietta Gay Simmons. The paper listed the cause of the woman's death as blunt force trauma. Police had yet to determine person or persons responsible in the case.

Beverly Jane came storming in as soon as she heard the children were present at my most recent body find. "It's a wonder that my children aren't traumatized by the whole experience!"

Gerald, the ever-present father figure, pulled up his trousers and asserted himself in our hen house. "Now, your mother wasn't to blame here. You know she didn't do it on purpose, Beverly Jane. Settle down."

She simmered as she stood there, arms crossed over her chest, tapping her foot.

Lucy turned to the obituary section of the paper and began reading all the accomplishments of Henrietta. "They gave her a quarter of a page, Mama. Lets' see – first woman ever to serve as Chairman of the Board of Education, the things we talked about and she served on several state committees. Did you know she helped to rebuild the Palace? Sounds impressive, Mama. I'm surprised she hasn't had a street or a bridge named after her by now."

"I'm sure she thought that to be a flagrant violation of social etiquette rules. It would be undignified, don't you think." I shook my head, knowing the woman lived and probably died "by the book of properness."

"Well, as a child, I used to wonder who George, Hancock, Broad and Pollock were, but now I know who and what the streets are named for." Beverly Jane seemed a bit mollified.

"Hold the paper still and let me read it with you."

"What else does it say, Lucy, anything interesting?" I asked.

"What's the McPherson Foundation?"

Beverly jumped on that. "McPherson was a big lumber man hereabouts in the mid 1900's. He never married and without children to spend all his money, he set up a trust for New Bern and the surrounding community to support education, the arts and special needs." She tugged the paper closer, "They helped homeowners rebuild down in Stonewall after that Hurricane Isabelle, remember? It says she was a new appointee to their board?"

Lucy pulled the paper back. "Yeah, says she served on several committees, but this year was the treasurer and clerk of administration. That sounds important."

"The McPherson Foundation gave money for several concerts and the theater group, I know for sure. I remember they recognized them at the Fourth of July celebration for contributing to the fireworks money." Beverly glanced over her sister's shoulders. "Look down here," she pointed to another article in the paper. "The lieutenant governor is on the same board. As chairman, he's calling for nominations for people who could fill her position."

"That seems fast. Don't they usually meet like twice a year, develop a budget and then delegate the monies?" Lucy added, "I never knew there was so much responsibility to being a board member."

"Wow, it says here the Foundation administers millions of dollars." Beverly pulled that section of the paper away from her sister. "They give away thousands each year. I wonder if it pays anything to be on their board. I know New Bern and its history. What are the qualifications for being a board member?"

"Well, since you aren't working today, the library would be a great place to start." I suggested. "You go find out. I've been known to serve on a few boards myself. Boo might be able to help you too, if they are open to recommendations."

Beverly Jane had lost her position with the Hatteras Yacht Corporation last year since the recession and was working part-time for the CSS Neuse Historical Society of Kinston. "I could become real interested if it pays anything." She grabbed up her sweater. "The library opens at 9 o'clock. I have to run. Mama, can you call Cousin Boo and see what she knows? Please."

Her antagonism forgotten, my daughter needed her mother after all. "Sure, as soon as I get breakfast put away." I turned to Gerald. "Are you going to the Dunkin this morning?"

"I was being useful here, or so I thought. Looks like you can hold the fort down now. Let me brush my teeth and I'm off." Gerald meets with a group of retired men every morning to discuss game scores, local politics and down a few donuts and cups of coffee. "I'll be back around noon. We can eat leftover pot roast if you've a mind."

"Open pot roast sandwiches it is. Lucy, are you staying another day?"

"I better get home, but I'll be back for the funeral, Mama. Let me help you with the breakfast dishes."

Chapter 10

The following week Gerald, Sam, Lucy and I attended the memorial services for Ms. Henrietta. Christ Church was packed, standing room only in the back. Folding chairs tucked into the side spaces between the wall and pews barely left room to pass. Some late attendees shuffled into another room where they could hear the service on relayed speakers.

The rector led us through the Book of Common Prayer, then introduced several prominent officials, including the mayor, who gave testimonies to the devotion and dedication Henrietta displayed during her lifetime. As an antiquated woman hobbled to the podium to give her praises for the deceased, Gerald leaned over and whispered, "Is it me or is it hot in here?" I saw perspiration on his forehead as he lifted his tie and collar, indicating his discomfort.

My jacket was sticking to my back, despite the cooler outside temperature. "The air conditioner must not be working." I whispered back, fanning with the funeral bulletin.

If I leaned forward in my seat, I could see Trey Barnes comforting Etti G on the front row. His arm held her close and her head occasionally brushed his shoulder. Etti G was wearing a long strand of pearls and a black lace dress. Her hair folded into a perfect French twist with a pearl-topped hair pick. Her father, Peter, sat stoically beside them. His head nodded every time someone mentioned an occasion that must have meant something to him.

Behind them sat Trey's father, WD Barnes, II, the Lt. Governor and the man called Dixon. I shuddered remembering their overheard conversation in the Bank of the Arts vault.

Had they been talking about Ms. Henrietta? What had she found out about Etti G's future father-in-law? I couldn't pay attention to the litany of good remembrances because I was thinking about all the possibilities. When the sermon concluded, we stood, sang a parting hymn and bowed for the benediction.

A long serpentine column of cars, headlights blinking, followed the hearse away from the church. We pulled into the limousine procession and drove to the out of town cemetery. Gerald parked off the highway and we picked our way among the tombstones to the green canvas tent and fake carpet of grass beneath it.

I couldn't help myself. At the graveside, I walked as close as I dared to the two government officials whom I overheard talking at the Bayard Wootten exhibit. Gerald grabbed my arm.

"Where are you going?" Trying to read my mind, Dear Husband tugged me to the side.

I fibbed, "I want to see better. You stay here in the shade and I'll be back in a minute." I stumbled over a tree's roots, caught myself and stood behind a large stone monument. As I eased my way into a better position, Boo hustled forward.

"What are you up to?" Her narrowed eyes told me she knew, for sure, what I was thinking and only wanted to confirm it. "You think they are going to gloat at her funeral, if she's who they talked about that day."

"Shush, they'll hear you." I shook my head and backed away. "I thought I might overhear something else." As we walked back to the shade where Gerald stood, I said, "I don't know whether I should mention it all to the police."

"What?" Gerald questioned me. His eyes narrowed. "You aren't getting involved in this. Not again."

"Well, I may as well tell you, honey. Don't be upset with me." I explained the conversation I overheard about them wanting to get rid of someone and seeing both men immediately intercepted by the deceased at the door of the Bank of the Arts.

The milling crowd of attendees who were finding their way back to their cars caused him to keep his voice down, but Gerald's face turned red. He all but spit out his response. "You're accusing WD Barnes of murdering Ms. Henrietta? Do you think the police will even listen to you? Why, you could be sued for libel or whatever they call it!" He shook his head like an angry bull. "Fiona, you will do no such thing. Can't you see this is distressing – our whole family."

It was true. Lucy stood beside him, chewing on her lip and frowning. "Mama, please don't start anything. Let's go home, change clothes and cool off. I can't face Etta G right now. Cousin Boo, we still have some of those brownies left. Want to join us?"

"We aren't going to their home for the wake?" She looked disappointed.

I encouraged her, "You go on there and tell me all about it later."

BEAR WITH ME, DEAR

House Number 7

The afternoon sun warmed us as we sat on deck chairs and watched the rivers. We had time to change into jeans and cotton shirts. The color of Gerald's face was back to normal. I nibbled on my brownie as I drank my coffee.

Lucy chewed a hangnail and grumbled, "Well what are you going to do, Mama?

"I don't know what I'm going to do."

She gnawed at her finger tip.

"Stop that! You'll tear off a cuticle and it will bleed. Go in our bathroom and get some clippers. Cut it off if that's bothering you."

Lucy's face turned red, tears formed in her eyes. She hopped up. I could hear her rummaging through the drawer in our bathroom cabinet. The sound of the nail clipper snipping in the next room stopped, but Lucy didn't return.

Sam got up and said, "I'll go see if she's alright." Sam met Lucy at college. They married as soon as she graduated. He works for a bank in Swansboro and had been promoted several times since they moved there from a little town close to the SC border. Sam usually wears Weejuns or deck shoes with his casual Friday clothes. His sandy blond hair, green eyes and slender build make him look like a college student. Being the son of a coastal fisherman, he had an island brogue but dropped that in college. His deeply grounded family values endear him as a favorite son-in-law.

Not that I don't like Bart, but Bart is a lot like Beverly Jane. Sometimes I wish they'd leave the starch out of their drawers. I sat there comparing our life and the lives of our children. My mind wandered over to child number two, Han Wade, whom we hadn't seen in a while. We named him for another uncle, Hancock Wade, but called him Han.

"What are you thinking?" Gerald tuned in to my thoughts.

"I was thinking about Han. He's been home from Afghanistan four months and we've only seen him once since then. Why don't we get the whole family here for my birthday? I want to see all my grandchildren." I had four counting Han's stepson. I hoped for more.

The door softly slammed downstairs and I saw Sam and Lucy walk in the direction of the riverfront. "Did I say something wrong to her?"

"No, you were just being a mama. Whatever is bothering her will surface eventually." He reached over and patted my shoulder.

"Well, what else can I be? I hurt when they hurt."

Gerald hugged me close. "Good, I was afraid you were trying to solve another murder. I'd rather talk about our wonderful children. Yes, we could invite everyone here for the day. Cook out? Or you want to take them all to Outback for a meal?"

"A cookout would be nice, but why not have Smithfield cater it? The weather will be warmer in April. Now we have to plan what we'll do with everyone." I thought for a moment. "You know what would be fun? We now have over 50 bears all around town." They were sponsored by different organizations, painted by local artists and finished off by an auto body shop so they wouldn't be damaged by sunlight or abuse. "Let's have a bear hunt!"

"How's that?"

"We'll go see all the bears around town."

"OK, that sounds like fun. I'll go to the visitors' center and get the Bear Hunt Maps, and we'll divide up into teams and see which team can find the most answers in an hour," he volunteered.

"You do that. We might want to make it longer than an hour, though."

"Don't they get prizes for answering questions on the maps anyway? What is it, a cookie or an ice cream cone?" My husband licked his lips thinking about those prizes.

"Yes, but we'll do something in addition to that. Here, let me get out my notepad and start making us a list. Now I have to call everyone first and make sure the date is open….."

House Number 8

Chapter 11

"Is Lucy here?" Wearing denim leggings and a gauzy ruffled top, Etti G stood at our front door again. "Don't tell me she has already gone home?" She looked around the yard. "Lucy's yellow Mustang isn't here."

"I'm afraid she's gone. She plans to come back for your wedding. Is that what this is all about?" I didn't mean to pry, but I could at least offer my help.

"Oh, Daddy wants to delay it, but Trey and I don't want to do that. I mean the invitations are already printed, stamped and mailed." She blinked her baby blues at me. "I even used those pretty little love flowered stamps they have at the post office. It took me a week to address and get them all ready." She leaned her pony-tailed head against the front porch post. "I just don't know what to do. I have my dress and the groomsmen's tuxedos ordered. Why there's the flowers and, OH LORDY, the reception at the Country Club." She was now wringing her hands. "I can't - can't call off another wedding."

As I invited her into our house, I smelled a hint of alcohol on her breath. "Sit here and tell me what the problem is as you see it."

"Why, it's Daddy!" She pulled a tissue out of her purse. "He doesn't think it would be proper. Well, WD, you know Trey's daddy says to go ahead. He won't mind any little wedding gossip.

"Do you know he even flew over to Bermuda last week to make sure all the arrangements for our honeymoon were perfect? He's such a sweet man." She blew her nose and tucked the tissue back in her purse.

"Really? My goodness. He went all the way over there, to be certain all the details were settled?"

"Well, just between you and me, I think he had some business to deal with. Once when I was in his office with Trey, I saw a bunch of business letterheads on his desk with international lettering. I think he has a condo or something over there."

"I see. Well, let's look up what Emily Post suggests, as options for a wedding after a funeral, shall we? I know your grandmother was very particular on what was proper."

"Oh yes, she was always very proper." She huffed a bit. "Sometimes I think she was too proper. We can't do anything society would think improper."

She crossed her fingers as I reached behind her on the shelf and pulled out my laptop computer. "Everything is online these days," I explained as I booted it up.

I consulted several online sites for appropriate functions and concluded, "Well, there are three for go ahead, one definite no and the third option is to reduce the pomp of the affair. Which can you live with? Or rather which do you think your daddy would agree to?"

"I'm using Janelle Foster as my wedding planner. I'll go see her now and maybe between the two of us we can get Daddy to agree to let me go ahead." She stood up and flipped her ponytail over her shoulder. "Thank you so much, Mrs. Wade. You were a terrific help. I already feel better. I'm sure Nana would approve of whatever we come up with." Etti G gathered her purse and turned to leave. I followed her out the door.

"Did you get a new car?"

Etti G stood still for a moment and then gave her head a quick spin. Her ponytail demurely wrapped around her neck. Her hand went up to tug it. "Oh, I had to take it into the shop. It wasn't running right. Besides, Trey said if I wanted a new one, he'd get me this car. Isn't it cute? I always wanted a convertible, but Nana didn't approve."

"Well, it certainly looks smart. Lucy loves her little yellow car. She says it makes her happy to drive it."

The girl looked astounded for two blinks of an eye. "Yes, I guess this car makes me feel happy too." She climbed into the new Thunderbird and waved goodbye as she pulled out of my yard.

I called Boo at work and she said she'd meet me at Stingray's for lunch. On Friday, they make fish stew. She was waiting on the corner when I walked across the street. We looked in the new bike shop and then went into the restaurant. The hostess seated us in a booth in the back.

Boo slid into her side of the table and said, "What's up? You don't usually call for lunch unless you want to bounce something off me."

"Well, I declare. Can't we just have a girlfriend lunch without you accusing me of collusion?"

Boo shook her head. "Give it up. I know you too well."

"Oh, alright."

The waitress came and took our orders.

"I'll have tea, half and half and a bowl of fish stew. On the side I want a half dozen steamed oysters."

Boo said, "What's half and half?"

"You know. You order sweet tea but half is unsweet. The waiters know what I mean."

"I'll have the same, but without the oysters." She looked at me with a raised eyebrow. "Oysters, huh?"

"I happen to like them and this is one of the last months we can get them fresh. So get your mind out of the gutter." I popped my straw out of the wrapper and stirred my tea with it. "Something has come up that makes everything more interesting." I took a deep breath. "Like I was telling you, I was --- but you never told me about the wake at the Simmons' home. Anything suspicious happen that you noticed?"

Boo frowned. "Lots of flowers. I never like the smell of carnations, do you? The white lilies were magnificent and the food!"

"Focus, Boo."

"Oh well, then. I observed and felt like Mata Hari, thanks to you. I sneaked around the flowers and food tables and tried to hear conversations between the persons," she made rabbit ears with her fingers, "of interest." They scooted into a corner close to the fireplace and kept their heads together for about five minutes. Then, that fellow you called Dixon, left as if someone held a torch to the front of his pants."

"Well, I would have paid money to be that gold clock above the mantel while they were talking." I leaned over the table to talk better in confidence. "Etti G told me this morning that her future father-in-law flew to Bermuda this week. Don't lieutenant governors have to keep office hours? Moreover, was he flying on our money and time? Humph."

House Number 9

"Wow, that is interesting hear-say. So where are you going with this?" Boo stirred her tea with her straw. "It's still all circumstantial. I don't work in an attorney's office and not pick up on the words." Her fingernail snapped on the polyurethane tabletop. "Ouch!" She reached into her purse and pulled out a nail file. "Don't you just hate it when you break a nail?" She gently filed the offending nail. "Anyway, unless you get hard evidence, no policeman will be interested in it."

"I know."

The waitress refilled our tea glasses after she brought us our meals. "Y'all need anything else? Want more hushpuppies?"

Boo replied, "No, thank you, Sugar. We're fine." She added pepper to her stew after tasting it. "Well, we have all this maybe-might'a, if-n-so suppositions and nowhere to take it. Can I have a couple of your oysters?"

I spooned a couple in her bowl and dumped the rest in my stew. "My daddy used to make it just like this after a day of fishing. It's good and this is the way I like it."

"I'm thinking campaign fraud, illegal use of public funds." Boo broke a hushpuppy into her stew and stirred the chunks of potatoes, fish and egg bits. "Now how do we go about proving it?"

"That's a good guess, about abuse of funds. I really want to go to Ron Meadows with what I know. Gerald says 'no,' but I really think we need to let someone hear what we have to say."

"What would Gerald say if we went to Ron's office and *I* told him what we know?"

"That might work. I really didn't want to make an official office visit about it since we aren't so official. Where do you think he eats his lunch?"

"Well, I know Sarah at the front desk over at the police station. Maybe I could give her a call."

Boo called me later that afternoon. We planned our 'informative' lunch the following day. Paula's Pizza is a favorite local Italian restaurant.

We caught the detective after his waitress set a large salad in front of him. He stopped shoveling a forkful of greens in his mouth long enough to give us a smile and motion us to sit with him for a bit. Boo started with the vault conversation and ended with the Bermuda trip, then leaned back in her chair.

"Say what?" Ron leaned over his garden salad. "You want me to question WD Barnes, the lieutenant governor?" He shook his head. "Better yet, the Lt. Governor and his administrative assistant? They'd have my badge!" He chomped on a giant mouthful of lettuce and tomato, shaking his head.

BEAR WITH ME, DEAR

Boo and I sat, watching him chew. I noticed he dropped a bit of honey mustard dressing on his navy striped tie, but I wasn't going to tell him. Ron is red haired, freckled and skinny. I wondered if, as a child, he had the Howdy Doody look. Of course, he is too young to know the marionette, Princess Summer Fall Winter Spring or Buffalo Bob. Oh, well, he probably watched Sesame Street. He still wasn't giving us any real consideration. Today his military-cut hair severity cut into his sweet looks.

"Mrs. Wade, Ms. Waters, I appreciate the information, but would you let me do my job? Now get on back there to your table and y'all enjoy your lunch and let me enjoy mine."

I apologized and we left him to his greenery.

Boo and I returned to our table and started our meal. "Ok, we did what we were required to do as good civic-minded women." She twirled hot Stromboli mozzarella cheese on her fork.

"I don't understand how you can stay so thin and eat like that. Now, quit playing with your food." I was miffed about the entire lunch predicament. "Eat what you ordered."

"Maybe the reason I'm so thin is because I do play with my food instead of gobbling it down, dear Cuz'n. Besides, you're only upset because he didn't take us seriously." She was right.

"I'm sorry. There's something so wrong with this picture. I can't connect all the dots exactly as they should be. Something is still wrong."

"Let's talk about something else. When are all the family getting together for this Great Bear Hunt you and Gerald are planning?"

"Ok, we'll drop the mystery for now. Let me tell you what we have planned so far.

"You're coming aren't you? I want you to be one of the team leaders. I'm splitting the family into three teams by drawing names. Beverly was always so competitive, so you, she and I are the team captains. One child goes with each team. It will be the child's responsibility to find all the clues.

"The adults can only drive, walk or answer any questions the child asks." I finished my pizza slice and tea. "The questions are about each statue's artist or colors or something that is painted on each bear or its base."

"So you are just going to leave this other? I mean this mystery of Ms. Henrietta.

You aren't going any further?" She turned her head and nodded as Ron Meadows paid his bill and left. "You are really through?"

"What else can I do - at this time? I have no more leads and haven't a clue to where to go next."

"Well, I'll be a *cross-eyed* bear! I never thought you'd give it up this easily."

Little did she know.

BEAR WITH ME, DEAR

Chapter 12

That evening when Beverly Jane came to collect the children, she asked, "Mama, want to go on one of your long evening walks with me?"

Beverly Jane never asks me to go on a walk. I nearly missed my cue. "Sure, when?"

"Right now."

She looked down at her two inch-heeled pumps and pulled her long hair up off her neck. "Give me ten minutes and I'll meet you at our back door. Daddy, can you listen out for the children? We shouldn't be gone more than an hour."

"Sure, Hon. No problem. Let them know I'm here if they need me, but I'm not settling any Doodle Head name-calling arguments. Only come get me if blood or smoke is involved."

Years of living with my Dear Husband have taught me about his "sensitivity and fairness," or lack thereof. Gerald shook out the morning paper and then folded the paper to the Scramblegram he'd yet to do.

Beverly left and Gerald eyed me. "What do you suppose that is all about?"

"I don't know, but we will find out, won't we?" I went upstairs to find my walking shoes and then put on my light windbreaker. I also put some lip-goo on my lips. I've always suffered from chapped lips, even as a girl.

Beverly was waiting for me when I went outside. Late March is breezy and the winds whipped off the river as we walked. She had changed into pressed khaki slacks and her Weejuns for walking. She tied a floral scarf around her neck. A fancy wooden clip caught up her hair. "Thanks for coming, Mama. I'm in a stew about the McPherson Foundation." She rambled on about her research at several web sites and in the library. She slowed her walk as she told me what she discovered about the charity. "I called some people who work there and they aren't looking for anyone with my qualifications. Right now, they want a part-time secretary and that's minimum salary. I did some additional digging. You know you can go on the web and research charitable organizations, tax exempt licensing and things like that, don't you?" She waited for me to nod. "They have this whole site about scams in the state and what to avoid, but what I found was interesting in my way of thinking."

"I never thought to look for any of that."

"Well, you have both the Secretary of State looking out for fraud and the Attorney General's office online.

"Anyway I wanted to see who all gets the grants and the processes they go about and who all has benefited for the monies. I really had a time worming my way around some corners and gobbly-gook verbiage. Attorneys sure know how to confound the general public."

House Number 10

We crossed the street at the traffic circle and continued up East Front Street. I watched where I stepped, not wanting to sprain my ankle. Beverly outpaced Boo. I never realized she had such a fast walk. I admired the crocuses and daffodils that were pushing up in sidewalk flowerbeds.

"So what exactly were you looking for?"

"I don't know. I thought if anyone interviewed me, I should be on my toes about what the foundation has done in the past and who gets the grants each year." She pulled a strand of hair from her face and tucked it behind her ear. "I thought if they needed a part-time person perhaps it could lead into something full time like an administrative assistant or even executive director. If there was any kind of possible future, I might be interested." She hopped across a stream of water from where the firemen were flushing a hydrant. I walked around it.

"So, did you find out anything helpful?"

"I don't know." We turned onto Queen Street, passed the Salvation Army Store and then we walked up North Craven Street. The homes on this street were built at the end of the 19th and beginning of the 20th centuries.

"On the Secretary of State website, you can investigate all these corporations and see the officers and what their business objective is like if it's a charity and who benefits. Interesting information if you know what you are looking for. I didn't really know. I only started by browsing."

Most of the homes along the street were in disrepair, but a few appeared to have new owners who were trying to bring up their appearances. Some were rentals in a barely livable state and others stood deserted. We continued walking, avoiding potholes in the road. "Stop, right here and tell me what you think."

"This house? It's boarded up. Recently added plywood, but it doesn't look like it's been lived in for years."

"Exactly." She checked a list of addresses in her pocket. "That's what I thought. But look at that one there, too." She pointed to another home in worse shape than the first. Someone had applied a whitewash sparingly to the outside. "That house received $145,000 in grant money and there were some details about an application for a tax credit for the refurbishing. I read the board minutes for last year." She continued to lead me down the block and pointed out two more homes. Leggy weeds thrust through some porches. Holes in the roof showed an earlier century's construction crisscross of beams.

"And this monstrosity is supposed to be an office that manages the redevelopment of the homes listed on this paper." She held a handwritten note out to me.

"Are you sure? Maybe you got the address wrong. Where did you get these numbers?" I continued to look at the unpainted two-story houses that had seen better times in the early 1900s. A toppling silo on the other side of the street towered over a vacant lot. A broken chain link fence leaned inward, keeping only the halfhearted vagrants away. Through the trees, I could see the Neuse River rounding another curve in the river that came down to the coast from Raleigh. "This is a strange place for a corporate headquarters." I walked over to the deserted building and peered on tiptoe into a crack between the plywood and a rotten windowsill. "Nothing in there. I smell varnish or something. There's a pile of rags on the floor."

"My thoughts exactly! I drove by here this afternoon. It was the first time I had a chance to find them. Mother, I think I found a problem with where some of this grant or foundation money has gone. I can't have gotten it all wrong, could I?"

"Let's go home and you show me how you got these addresses and what all is involved. Did you find who is on the board at the McPherson Foundation?"

"But don't you see. If someone is falsifying records, what's to keep them from arson? Most of these buildings can go up in smoke and there would be no great loss, except that the money documented for their repairs was never spent."

"Let's hope you made a mistake or maybe there's another North Craven Street in the county."

Tryon Palace Arbor

Beverly pulled another slip of paper from her pocket as we turned and walked away. "I found these names. Do you know any of them?"

Among the names were WD Barnes, Blair Dixon and Henrietta Gay Simmons. The addresses of other board members were in Raleigh, Charlotte and Valle Crucis, North Carolina. I read the names and addresses. "Spread out, aren't they?"

"Yeah, you'd think with the area of concern being here and the surrounding towns of New Bern that more board members would live closer. Maybe they do this to keep from playing favorites, like with the different communities. They don't want to personally be acquainted with the people, but judge the requests on an unbiased basis."

We continued walking down Craven Street back toward town. The architecture of the homes varied like the multi-colored tulips that sprang from their yards.

My suspicious mind fidgeted with the information. No resting, until I figured out what Beverly Jane had discovered or where she made her mistake.

By the time we arrived home, it was too late to do anything about the Foundation information. The grandchildren were squabbling. They needed feeding *and* their homework checked *and* the dog needed to be walked. Beverly Jane said she wasn't working on Thursday so I said I'd have time to look over her shoulder as we retraced her searches.

Gerald was patting hamburger patties into sizable shapes when I appeared. "I thought I'd get something started for supper. Can I grill these while you fix something to go with them?"

"Are we into WHOPPERS now?" I pulled a bag of sweet potato slices out of the freezer and sprayed cooking spray on a baking sheet. "I don't want a charcoal briquette by the time you've finished cooking mine. Cook all of them and we'll freeze what we don't eat. I can always use them in something else later. Want some broccoli, too?"

"A little orange, a little green and you want a little red?"

"I'd prefer pink in the center, dear." As I replaced the potato bag, I pulled out the broccoli and poured some water into a saucepan. "Interested in what my daughter discovered, or thinks she did?"

"Oh dear, this sounds like an antacid moment," he held his stomach. "She is *our* daughter, however. Hold the story until I get these quarter pounders on the grill."

As we ate, I told Gerald what I had learned that afternoon. "Those houses were nowhere near rehabilitated. They probably got some federal money too, as matching. You know if this has been done to more than Craven Street and they got away with it, then we are talking millions of dollars."

"Now, hold your horses. You don't know yet if any of this is accurate. We have to check our facts, Missy. Maybe she looked up the wrong things and the street addresses are somewhere else. You know they have done a lot of rebuilding homes in that area. Maybe you got some wrong information."

"It remains to be seen is all I can say. It remains to be seen."

Chapter 13

By the time Beverly and I rechecked all her addresses and names, I was certain there was a problem. Or rather, the lieutenant governor and Mr. Dixon were scheming or skimming monies from the McPherson Foundation. Both men were listed as officers of various limited partnerships and closed corporations in the documents. It took the determination of a bulldog to weasel our way through all the corporate jargon and connections.

I called Boo that evening to share my suspicions. "Ms. Henrietta probably found out what they were doing. If they tidied up their act, they had to do away with her. I wouldn't be surprised if some of these houses became arson prone in the coming month."

"They did what? You know not! Why they can't get away with that; surely there are checks and balances."

"I don't know what there are, but one thing I know for sure, is that someone needs to see this. I made copies of all the information Beverly and I discovered and even took pictures of the houses at the few addresses we had. Do you want to go with me? I'm going to sit in the police station until that Ron Meadows lets me into his office."

"I wouldn't miss his eating crow for anything. Count me in. I have a deposition to take in the morning, but I can get away around 10:30. I'll meet you there."

I called Ron, briefly explained my suspicions and asked for an appointment to show the evidence. He scheduled time for us. The next morning, Detective Meadows ushered

BEAR WITH ME, DEAR

Gerald, Boo and me into a conference room.
Another man rose to greet us. "This is Gillis
Williams of the SBI. I've been conferring with
him and believe he will be interested in what
you have to say."

The large African American held a chair
for me and we all sat at the worn wooden table.
My chair had a bit of a wobble. I tried to ignore
the tapping of the odd leg as I distributed copies
of our findings.

Boo adjusted her necklaces and then
clasped her purse in her lap. She looked like the
cover of Bazaar Magazine. My Dear Husband
leaned back in his chair and proceeded to push
his lips in and out, as he huffed little puffs of
air. He was not happy we'd gone this far with
the case.

Ron pushed a button on his recording
machine. I talked. Every now and then, as I

made a point, the SBI man licked his bottom lip.

Neither said anything. They looked at the papers and made notes as I continued to read from my observations. The SBI man used an electronic note pad while Ron jotted in his spiral notebook.

In conclusion, I said, "So what I think is, that Ms. Henrietta, being familiar with the properties, took WD to task and he killed her to keep her quiet!" I smiled at Boo. She smiled back and nodded her head in encouragement. Dear Husband pushed out his bottom lip and huffed.

"What do you think?"

"We think Henrietta Gay Simmons was killed sometime late Friday night and dropped off at the cemetery before daylight the next morning. I believe you have a motive, but unfortunately, both the gentlemen in question were in Raleigh on the days she was killed and laid out in the graveyard. " He nodded his head at me. "I did look into your initial information. That led me to Williams' investigation.

"We know she was killed the previous day and deposited that night. That would have her there by the time the Questers arrived as well as the other visitors, besides you and your grandchildren.

"Their alibis are stone tight as the House was in session. Both men were present in committee meetings from eight o'clock in the morning until late, both days." Ron Meadows tapped his pencil to his tablet. "The three hour drive to and from Raleigh would have been impossible with their schedules."

"Why that's crazy! Maybe they flew down." Boo leaned forward and pressed her forefinger into the tabletop. "Both those men had a reason to do her in, so to speak. They could have hired someone, even."

This time Mr. Williams spoke up, "We want to thank you for your determination in unraveling the funds we tracked into both men's offshore accounts. We were looking at campaign contributions and other political sources. Our unit suspected tomfoolery and had an ongoing investigation ever since Lt. Governor Barnes bought a place in the islands and sent both his children to Ivy League schools.

"Mr. Dixon, his accomplice in all this, has bought two Mercedes, one for himself and another for his wife -- and an expensive fur coat for a lady friend." He grinned. "I don't want to see his wife's tirade when she finds out, either. When the media gets a hold of this, the whole thing is going to explode." He shook his head back and forth. Being the size of Shaquille O'Neal, his comment about Mrs. Dixon's fury made me grin.

"We hadn't looked at the McPherson Foundation until you mentioned it to Detective Meadows." He glanced at the paperwork I prepared. "I have to say you did your homework."

"Dad-gum right she did." Gerald cleared his throat. "Fiona, once she gets started, does her homework!"

"Is there a reward for this?" Boo's eyebrows went up as well as the color in her cheeks.

"I can't say for certain, at this time. We'll need to verify this information; put our computer man on the threads you found and pin these two down.

"I'll need to talk to the DA and see what she wants to do and how to proceed here. You'll be kept in the fold, so to speak. Detective Meadows will contact you as needed, but we really need to keep this quiet for a few more days." He stood up, an indication that the conference was over.

"Humph!" Boo snorted and backed her chair away from the table. "Looks like they are shoving us out of the picture."

"That's fine with us, as long as justice is served." Gerald stood up and helped me gather my papers. "Want to grab some lunch at Bella Cucina, the new Italian restaurant on Trent Road?" That's my Dear Husband, always thinking about where the next meal is coming from.

"If you don't need us any longer, I guess we'll leave." I stood up and reached for my purse.

"Mrs. Wade," Ron reached over and held my hand. "It looks like you've done it again. You take all the fun out of my job if you do the investigating for me."

"Ron. Really, I don't mean to do this. I seem to stumble over things and then put them all together. It's just curious that it happens when *I* find a body! Let's hope you can find out who killed Ms. Henrietta while you are following the clues to the money drain." With that, I clasped his hand in both of mine and shook it.

"Boo, will you be joining us?" Gerald held the outside door for us.

"No, y'all go ahead and let me know how it is at that new place. I need to get back to the office. I hope when WD gets confronted by you two," she nodded at both police officers, "that he goes to some other attorneys' office. I don't want to have to look at the man after all this. I always liked the way Ms. Henrietta got things done. I'll miss her."

***

Gerald and I found a table at the new restaurant and ordered. "I don't like that you've done this again, Fiona. Maybe we need to think about some longer cruises come summer. I hear the Albemarle Sound has lots of little hidey holes we can creep up into and tie up or anchor. Would you like that? Columbia, Elizabeth City, do the loop around the Dismal Swamp, head out to Manteo? I'll stick to your side while we are cruising and we *will not* find any bodies along the way. I promise."

BEAR WITH ME, DEAR

"It's a deal, partner." The atmosphere surprised me as the new owners had pulled open the heavy drapery and let in the sunshine. The food was excellent.

Chapter 14

"Mama, can we come to your house for the weekend, stay over for your party and Etta G's wedding on Sunday?" Lucy called to arrange accommodations for herself and her husband, Sam.

"Certainly, we'd love to have you. But you sure you wouldn't rather stay with Beverly? Her house is bigger."

"No, I explained to her already I like having access to our own bathroom. Her guests have to share with the kids. One thing I don't want is three children and a dog nosing around my knees while I'm trying to do my hair in the morning."

"Sure, I'll make up the bed and have it ready." I surmised that when she did have children, her opinion of kids and dogs at her knees during her morning toilette would change. I turned to Gerald who was sipping his cup of coffee with me before he headed out. "Lucy and Sam will be spending the night with us come Friday. She is staying over to attend Etti G's wedding."

"Good, she and Sam can also help clean up after this party you are planning. Don't you think a bear birthday cake is a little much?"

"No, I still have the cake pan I had when Beverly Jane was a little girl. You like chocolate frosting, don't you? Yellow cake, too. We're going to pick up the rest of the food from Smithfield's so neither one of us has to cook. Cleanup will be swift."

"It's your cake and your party. Do whatever you want. I'm off." He kissed my cheek and grabbed the keys that hung on the door rack. "Don't go to any trouble for lunch. Sandwiches will do."

I checked the refrigerator after he left and saw we needed more than cake makings. I pulled my notepad out of the kitchen drawer and started listing everything we needed for the party. I knew I was going to be shopping all morning.

*****

Tuesday morning, before I could read the paper, Boo called. "Did you see it? They made the eleven o'clock news and this morning, too. Both our *persons of interest* are in the hoosegow!"

"Say what?"

"Jail! They arrested them last night. It won't be in the paper until tomorrow. Let's hope the reporter gets it all right. You had better call Beverly. The Foundation may need more than a part-time secretary, by the time this all blows over."

I flipped on the morning news with our remote and a series of commercials flashed by while I muted them. "Well, at least it's all out in the open. Poor Etti G's wedding may not happen after all. That poor girl. Bless her heart."

"Well, with everything else that has happened, knowing her, she may go ahead and do it! The father of the groom can be replaced, don't you think?"

"Boo, don't say that. Not when he killed Ms. Henrietta."

"Well, they aren't mentioning the murder at all in the news. Only the misuse of funds and there was a picture of our man Dixon's wife scrappling with his lady friend at the police station."

"Really! Hold on, here it comes." I clicked the voice on while a young reporter stood on the lawn of the courthouse and described the circumstances under which the SBI arrested the Lt. Governor. A light breeze blew through the young reporter's hair as he checked his iPad for notes.

Electronics were going to be my next undertaking; if some whipper-snapper news reporter could manage one, so could I.

"Under the guise of several corporations, Lt. Governor WD Barnes and his associate, Blair Dixon, abused their positions on the board of a local foundation. Taking money to supposedly rehabilitate a half dozen houses in New Bern and surrounding towns…" The camera flashed to several of the homes Beverly and I examined the first day of her discovery. The excited reporter briefed viewers of the information, then signed off.

"See, told you." Boo's voice brought me back. "Well, I must get to work."

"Ow! My hand holding the phone fell asleep as I clicked to other local stations and watched." I flipped out my fingers to get the blood circulating again.

"You take care, Sugar. Oh, by the way, can I bring Sid on Saturday, please? We usually have a standing date for Saturday and he'll be fun. He keeps me in stitches with his stories."

"Certainly. One more won't make a difference. Do you want him on your team?"

"No, no. Let him go where you pick him. I just wanted him to be included. Thanks, Sweetie. Gotta run."

I went outside to pick my white narcissus and perky yellow daffodils. As I bent over,

Beverly came out of the backdoor of her house. "I suppose you saw the news this morning."

"I just watched it for a few minutes. No new news - as far as I could tell. I'm proud of you, the way you researched all that information. If you hadn't been interested, all that might have been shoved under the table without any further notice."

"Thanks, Mother, but I didn't mean to stir up any pot of problems for anyone." She shook her head. "Have you got everything under control for this weekend? Han and Loretta are coming up on Friday night. Sean can sleep in Bart's room. Lucy tells me she and Sam are staying with you."

"Yes, I'm getting so excited. Hold this for me." I gave her the crystal vase my mama gave me on our wedding day and plopped a few stems inside it. As I cut, she bent to help retrieve the blooms.

"How about if I cook breakfast for everyone over here? It's been a long time since we all ate at Granny's dining room table. It will be fun. I'll even use the good china."

I slid the last bloom into the arrangement and took the vase from her. "That sounds wonderful. We'll be busy getting lunch picked up, the party favors given out and directions ready. May I invite Boo and her friend, Sid, too?"

She threw up her hands and smiled, "Why not? Now let me go inside and make a list of everything I'll need."

That's my girl. I think list making is in our genes.

"Do you have any of your dinner rolls in the freezer, Mom?"

"I don't think so; buy Sister Schubert's. They're good." The fragrance of the flowers made me smile. The original bulbs planted generations ago by my grandmother now stretched as a border across the back yard. "These are wonderful." I held the vase so she could take a big whiff.

"Hmm, lovely." She returned my smile.

"Promise me you'll never dig these up and do away with them."

"I may give some to my daughters when they have a home of their own, if that's alright."

"It would make me very happy if you did. Well, I have things to do."

"Need anything at the store?"

"I went yesterday, thanks." I don't think my feet touched the grass as I headed to my door. This arrangement with Beverly living in my front yard might help us to grow closer together after all. I quickened my step hearing the phone ring.

"Mrs. Wade, this is Ron Meadows. Did you catch the news this morning?"

"Yes, but Henrietta wasn't mentioned. I was sure you'd arrest them for that too. I'm disappointed."

"Well, we nailed them good, thanks to you and your daughter, but they aren't budging on any overheard conversation about doing away with that woman. Phone records and cash transfers show no sizable chunks going anywhere but to their own accounts. I'm not so sure they had anything to do with her death."

"Well, just thinking it - in my book, makes them guilty."

"They did admit that Mrs. Simmons had discovered one of the house grants to be a fake. She threatened that if they didn't make it right, she would bring in a prosecutor. That woman had no idea of the scope of their betrayal to the Foundation. I'm sure she would have discovered it all if she had lived long enough." Someone interrupted him. "I need to go. I wanted to be sure that you knew what was going on. Officer Williams called me this morning and we talked a bit. He asked me to call you."

"Thanks, Ron. Give my best to your mother. I don't think it's all over yet." I hung up, but my mind dredged up new suspicions.

BEAR WITH ME, DEAR

Chapter 15

Saturday's breakfast was the best surprise ever. Beverly invited Quinn and Charles to join us. That brought our total party to 16. Quinn made cinnamon rolls that we reheated. Beverly fixed scrambled eggs and fried livermush, a favorite of mine. I don't know where she found the livermush, but it tasted like my Granny's. The grandchildren preferred the bacon and sausage. Most of the conversation recalled events that filled the house when Quinn and I were children, memories of the past.

As we cleared the plates, I outlined the program for the day, "We'll break up into four teams of four each for our bear hunt. Each team will have one grandchild and three adults." While some helped to wash the breakfast dishes, I drew the names for the teams. Gerald took Charles off to get a glimpse of our boat before they picked up the lunch. Quinn went with them.

I made a list of the teams. On Boo's team were Sean, Lucy and Loretta, who is Han's wife. Sid, Grace and Sam were members of my team. Beverly had Gerald, Charles and the Bartlet. Quinn kept her team of Big Bart, Han and Gerri on task. I gave out the maps and the clues. Each team exchanged cell phone numbers so we could keep up with one another.

My team headed to Union Point Park to count buttons on Bearon DeGraffenried's coat before crossing over to the bears that line the walkways around the convention center.

Boo loaded all her team in Big Red, her Cadillac, to chase down Tabearna Bear, Travelin'Bear at Bridgepoint Hotel and the Marine Corps Bear, Semper Fi, at the airport. Beverly put everyone in her Pacifica and took off to find Bearon de Wilbur Forestry Bear, Walt, the "Mr. Safety" Bear and Super Agent, the Bearon de Broker.

I led my group down to the waterfront to check off all the bears along the Riverwalk. Grace snapped pictures of all her bears on our journey. As we passed the Hilton, a huge truck backed onto the lawn and deposited a tall spruce tree in a burlap wrap. "Well, what in the world?" I asked.

"Oh, you didn't hear the story of how the city workmen undecorated the Christmas tree in January." Sid scratched his chin.

I looked around trying to remind myself where the tree had been located.

"Yes-siree, Ms. Henrietta, God rest her soul, had that tree brought here specifically to plant for the community sing and tree-lighting at Christmas. Had it brought in from the North

Carolina mountains, as I recall it." One eye winked shut in his determination to remember correctly.

I recalled the tall evergreen lit up last Christmas during a community sing. A crew in a cherry picker truck had strung lights all the way to the top.

"Well, as I was saying, the city hired some part-time workers to do the after holiday cleanup. You know take down the wreaths and lights from all the light poles around town and on the Trent River Bridge and store them away." He took his handkerchief out of his back pocket and blew his nose.

"Well sir," he nodded to Grace and Sam, "They did just fine. Took all the stuff back to storage, packed it all away and then someone told them to take down Ms. Henrietta's Christmas tree. Well, you see, not everyone knew how she felt about that tree, being the primary instigator of its planting and growth.

"She set up a little fund for the fertilizing, watering and whatever it took, throughout the year. She even paid to have it sprayed against insects that may attack its growth, herself, don't you know. That dear lady was unwavering about her tree's care. I'm sure she got the city board riled a time or two when she asked for the special waterline to be put in and for pruning it so it shaped up real pretty-like.

"Yes, we enjoyed these past five years with that tree all strung out with lights and the community sing with Santa coming and all. It sure was a sight."

Grace stood still eyeing the tree that leaned over on its side while a funnel shaped machine dug a hole in the ground. One man directed the digging making sure no water lines were cut. "Hey y'all. Come on. We gotta get going or they will beat us back," she said.

Sid gave the tree one last look back and Sam followed. "Let me tell you, when Ms. Henrietta found out those boys took a chain saw to her tree, you'd 'a thought Mt. Vesuvius erupted again!" He coughed in his handkerchief again as we crossed the street to the Farmers' Market to snap a photo of Harvest Bear.

"Yes sir, who would have thought those newcomers would literally *take the tree down* when all they supposed to do was take off the lights!"

Sam chuckled and took out the pencil to write while Grace listed all the farm-grown veggies on the bear in plaid shirt and overalls.

"Just telling you like it is, you know." Sid jammed his hands in his pockets and followed along. "Hey, Miss Gracie, I believe I see another bear up there on Middle Street."

We ticked off the downtown bears by the hour's end and returned to home to take a car out where the other bears were known to stand. On our way, we picked up Freedom Bear and Barrister Bear on Pollock Street.

Sam drove his SUV for me. Sid Livingston's long legs weren't crunched in Sam's front seat. We rode comfortably rather than my little Toyota. Sam turned left on Pembroke Road to find the Bear D'Olde Towne. He parked the car on a street leading into the community and we all got out to see how many critters might be painted on the bear's pedestal.

"I see a turtle!" Grace took the sheet from Sam and wrote in the animal. "Huh, you can't see the frog, here. The bear is stepping on it." Without thinking, she shoved the statue over so she could look at the base. The bear wobbled and took a dive. "Oh, no! I didn't mean to do that." Both hands flew to her face, which turned white in fear.

"It's ok, honey. Something is wrong here if a stature topples over with a little shove." Sid looked at the base. His hand ran along the broken edge of the fiberglass, picking at the residue of the broken statue. "Look-a-here. You didn't do this little lady. It was already broke off and someone propped it back up here. See, you can see a dent and red paint where a car or something hit the legs with a mighty wallop. It must have been going pretty fast for that to pop off like that."

Sam kicked the turf with his shod foot. "Looks like it happened some weeks back, but you can still make out tire ruts here." He pointed to several ruts beneath the thick grass and ivy. "Well, I'll be. Would you look at that?"

My mind logged the color of the paint swipe, as my eyes followed the direction that his hand pointed. In the heavy foliage lay a navy blue thick-heeled shoe, Ms. Henrietta's missing shoe.

"Oh dear. This bear hunt is over." I reached in my pocket and pulled my cell phone out to call the others. I told everyone to stop where they were and meet us back at the house. I'd be there directly and then I dialed another number.

"911 operator. What is your reason for calling?" If I didn't know better, I'd say the same woman answered the phone as the last time I made the call.

"Well, maybe this isn't an emergency. I'm sorry to bother you, but I believe I've found evidence of who killed Ms. Henrietta Gay Simmons." She took the information and within another 15 minutes, a squad car pulled up at the entrance of Olde Towne. Then, I dialed Gerald and asked him to pick me up in thirty minutes.

Chapter 16

They ate lunch without us, but saved the cake cutting for when I got there. The children played a video game afterwards. I didn't say a word until all the grownups gathered around the dining room table. Some were picking through the fried chicken and barbeque pork left on trays on the table. I fixed myself a plate before starting.

"Don't hold anything back, Fiona. Tell us what's happening," Boo jumped in after she brought me a glass of sweet tea.

Beverly placed a tray of cut vegetables and dip on the table with a dish of salted nuts. "This is healthier grazing food." She eyed her husband.

"Well, I was wrong about WD and that Dixon. They hadn't killed Ms. Henrietta.

"They were merely thieves, scoundrels with greed on their minds. Ms. Henrietta found out about it and I guess she wanted to stop the wedding. No proper Simmons could marry the son of a thief!

She must have been taking her evening walk when an inebriated granddaughter missed a turn heading home. Or, I'm sure that's what they will say."

Boo stated, "It takes a dedicated attorney with plenty of confidence and experience to defend a vehicular homicide. In addition, that girl tried to hide it all, too. That won't go well with the judge."

"Etti G sobered up quick enough to hide her grandmother," I continued, "and then talked her fiancé into helping her move the body. Trey must have really had second thoughts about marrying her after that, but I guess he was blinded by love or so it appeared.

"If I were him, I'd plead temporary insanity," Boo said.

"It's my understanding that the rehearsal dinner was interrupted tonight when Etti G, Trey and Peter Simmons were escorted to the jail. Peter wasn't involved. He wanted to be there for them. I'm sure he knows a few attorneys to call."

Lucy leaned forward. "No wedding, again." A frown replaced her usual sunny smile. "She sure has had a tough time."

"Well, she should have had help a long time ago, but Peter was too proud to put his daughter in rehab." Boo explained to Quinn and Charles.

"I remember her from school. She was always getting into trouble and she loved a party." Han shook his head explaining the tragic youth of Etti. "She wasn't going to slow down and no one could touch her, between her wealth and Ms. Henrietta's political pull. That grandmama of hers fought tooth and nail to keep her out of jail when they caught her driving under the influence the first time."

"That's what led to her demise, I'm afraid, but hey, don't we have a birthday to celebrate here?" Gerald popped a radish in his mouth and crunched it loud enough to get the children's attention. "Who won the BEAR HUNT, y'all?"

"We did," Bart exclaimed.

"No Bear Breath, you only got to 23 bears. We did 31!" Gerri pulled her answer sheet out of her pocket and showed it to me.

"That's nothing Bear Poop. We got 33 and I have pictures to prove it." Grace produced her digital camera and churned through the shots counting off as she went. "And we caught a murderer! Extra credit for that." She grinned at me.

"I can't argue with that proof," I said. "Let me get my bag of prizes."

Han interrupted us while I was digging through my bag, distributing gifts to all the children. "I have a surprise for you, too." He hugged Loretta to his side. "We are pregnant! Sometime in September. You're going to be a grandma again. How do you like that?" His grin took up his entire face.

"My Wild Child is going to be a father," I responded. "I only hope he turns out as good as you did."

"He may be a she, Mama. But if he is a he, if I can't straighten him out, I'll send him to the Corps." My Marine son grew up a lot when he joined the Corps. Even his wife was a former Marine.

Sean came over. "I'm going to be a big brother? Wow!" He turned to Gerri. "What's it like being the oldest?"

Grace butted in, "She gets away with murder! Oops, sorry, wrong word." She eyed me. "Sorry, Grandma. She gets away with a lot and she doesn't have to wear hand-me-downs!"

"Shut up, Twirp. Come on y'all let's finish this game and then I'll race you to the swings across the street in the park."

Beverly touched her older daughter's shoulder, "Watch out for your brother and sister while you're over there."

"Sure, Mom." Gerri turned back to Sean. "And you get a lot of *responsibilities*, too. Oh brother!"

We laughed as the children fled.

***

My birthday was the best one that I could remember and probably it will be the most remembered. Lucy and Sam called the following week.

"Hi, Mom, how was your day?" I could feel her smile through the conversation.

I told her about planting my spring flowers and the walk I took and then she got very quiet. "How was your day, Sweetheart?"

"Well, I wasn't feeling so good and I made an appointment to see my doctor last week. I went today.

She whooped, "We're having a baby, too, Mama. Tell me how soon I will get over this nausea?" I heard Sam snicker in the background.

"Wait a minute. Let me tell your Daddy." I turned to Gerald. "We will be doubly blessed this year. Lucy is pregnant, too."

"Well I'll be. Tell her I'm pleased. I know she will make a wonderful mama." Gerald got up from his recliner to listen to her voice in the receiver.

"Oh, Daddy, I'm so nervous. Hey, I almost forgot to tell you. I got the strangest call from Etti G today. She's returning my gift and while she is out on bail, she is attending some alcoholic rehab program. I hope she makes it."

"You have other things more important to worry about now, sweetheart. Think about your baby and your business and your growing family."

"Yeah, I'm gonna do that, Mama. Love you and Daddy. Bye now."

We said our goodbyes and hung up.

Gerald nuzzled my cheek, "Love you, too." He slapped the cruising guide on the counter. "We better plan our cruise for early summer. It sounds like we'll have a busy fall."

Houses   Addresses

1-

2-

3-

4-

5-

Houses   Addresses

6-

7-

8-

9-

10-

Here's a hint. Walk the same streets as Fiona.

Email me at <u>kedodd2@yahoo.com</u> with the house numbers and the correct addresses of each house. Tell me the name of the book you'd like. We'll contact you to deliver the book.

See my website for the names and a brief description of each book. <u>www.karenedodd.net</u>

Carolina Comfort   ISBN 0-9707197-4-4

Carolina Comfort II   ISBN 0-9707197-2-2

Down East on Nelson Island   ISBN 978-07197-3-7

Begin Again, Quinn ISBN 978097197-5-1

Shifting Sands   ISBN 978097097-6-8

Riverwalk Mysteries

Spirit of Union Point ISBN 978097197-7-5

Dead Beat at the Palace ISBN 978097197-8-2

Bear With Me, Dear ISBN 978-0-9707197-9-9